THE IRON
CHILDREN

THE IRON CHILDREN

REBECCA FRAIMOW

SOLARIS

First published 2023 by Solaris
an imprint of Rebellion Publishing Ltd,
Riverside House, Osney Mead,
Oxford, OX2 0ES, UK

www.solarisbooks.com

ISBN: 978-1-78618-988-2

A CIP catalogue record for this book is available from the
British Library.

Designed & typeset by Rebellion Publishing

This one's for the Snekfruits.

ASHER AND SOR Elena had been on the road with their unit of Dedicates for a week now. Asher had tried not to have expectations for how it would be. She had never been near a battle before in her life. Many of her schoolmates had enlisted in the Cesteli infantry as soon as they turned fourteen; while they went off to the front lines, Asher had spent the last five years behind the walls of a Holiest House, learning strategy, theology, scientific soteriology, and all the other subjects that formed the curriculum of a Cesteli Sor-Commander.

Asher was not naive enough to believe her lessons could prepare her for the reality of war—but so far, her duties on the march had been almost shockingly routine. Every morning Asher assisted Sor Elena with her standard self-maintenance: removing any dirt or grit that had worked its way inside the copper and iron of the Sor-Commander's carapace, and ensuring that any minor mechanical damage was resolved before it could worsen. Then Asher and Sor Elena mounted their mules for the day's travel while the Dedicates got into marching formation behind them. When they stopped, Asher rubbed down the mules, then used the last of the dying light to study maps of the terrain ahead. Once her duties were taken care of, she left Sor Elena meditating by the road and crawled into her own small tent to sleep. Sor Elena, of course, did not sleep anymore.

The Dedicates did sleep, but they generally pitched their own tents a respectful distance away and took care of their own food and maintenance. They were not as vulnerable to environmental damage as Sor Elena— their carapaces were overlapping plates of uniform dark mail, all heavy practicality with none of the handcrafted filigree and fanciful flourishes that the sisters who took the soul's habit forged for themselves. But unlike their Sor-Commanders, somewhere beneath all that featureless iron they had a pulse, and a heartbeat.

Somehow, that made them feel stranger to Asher than the habited sisters.

But that was just unfamiliarity—or so Asher told herself, watching the gray hulk that was Sergeant Barghest come marching up from the Dedicates' encampment for the regular evening briefing. Asher had now spent hundreds of hours studying under Sor Beatriz's unchanging crystal eyes; she'd taken apart Sor Rafael's arm and put it back together again, while Sor Rafael watched and critiqued her technique. The Dedicates in training at the Holiest House, however, had their own wing of the building, separate from the novices. They ate their own food and learned from their own instructors and marched around the training grounds all in a line, walking in step like the automatons they weren't. They did not fraternize with the novices who would become their commanders.

In theory, Asher understood the military logic behind this. In practice, the Dedicates were specifically designed to be intimidating, and perhaps the sisters who had designed them that way might have considered the combination of these factors—but that was why Sor Elena included her in these regular meetings with the Sergeant to begin with. Asher was already growing used to them. By the time they reached the front lines, five days hence, the Dedicates wouldn't discomfit her at all.

"How are the troops, Sergeant?" asked Sor Elena, as the Dedicate approached.

Barghest saluted and gave the same response as always: "The troops are well."

Sor Elena turned to Asher. "Novice? The terrain report?"

Asher straightened her back and launched into her prepared analysis. "Tomorrow's route will be challenging. We're moving from the flatlands up Green Adam's lower slopes. In some places the path has a sharp drop to one side, so everyone should be cautious. And we don't have the latest measurements on how far down the ice descended this year. That may make the footing unpredictable."

She became aware that she was attempting to emulate Sor Elena's artificially even tones, and coughed, slightly embarrassed. Her voice had an unfortunate tendency to go up at the ends of sentences, but better that than sound like she was pretending to a status that she hadn't yet attained.

"There may be some seismic activity, too. Green Adam's known for tremors. But if we make good time, we can get through the worst of it and be on the downslope again to make camp? And then of course the other risk is the cold. Sergeant—"

She broke off. The Dedicates' legs and upper arms had human bone and muscle under their armor, but they also had a set of artificial lower arms that were godstone-animated clockwork like the sisters' habits. Freezing could be a problem for the oiled joints of the habited sisters, and perhaps the Dedicates' mechanical arms were susceptible to the same risks, but Sergeant Barghest almost certainly knew more about that than she did.

"Your medical officer can advise on the appropriate procedures, Sergeant," Sor Elena cut in smoothly. "Novice Asher is correct, however, that frostbite is a risk to be avoided." Sor Elena inclined her head, and Asher glowed inwardly. She was fairly sure she had passed another test.

The glow faded a little, as she looked back at Sergeant Barghest. Even though Sor Elena's face never changed, it was easy to read approval in the graceful serenity of her copper face and the steady glimmer of her gemstone eyes. Sergeant Barghest was an entirely different matter. A Dedicate's features were limited—eyes and mouth locked away behind a protective metal grille, the slats too close together to reveal anything behind them. Hard to read anything positive behind those grim bars; all too easy to see disapproval and doubt.

But, Asher reminded herself, Sergeant Barghest had only ever been polite and respectful. If she imagined any judgment in the Dedicate's face, it was her own judgment of herself reflected back at her.

"Thank you, Commander," said Sergeant Barghest, and saluted with their upper right arm. Their two mechanical arms stayed folded at their waist. In theory, their voice—formed with a broadly human throat, and ordinary vocal cords—should have sounded more expressive than Sor Elena's artificial pipes. In practice, they managed to achieve a tone that conveyed as little as the metal grille over their eyes.

They turned back towards the camp, their spine as straight as a tentpole. Or rather, Asher mentally amended, looking at her own slightly crooked tentpole, significantly straighter. She sighed.

"You needn't worry about impressing the Dedicates," Sor Elena said.

Asher jumped. "I'm sorry?" she said, and then, when her ears caught up to her mouth: "Oh, I—yes, of course. I didn't—I know that's not my job."

A soft whistle of sound came from Sor Elena's pipes. It could have been a chuckle, or an answering sigh. "The Dedicates follow my orders. Someday, these or others may follow your orders as well. What matters is your control over yourself—not what they think of you."

Asher nodded, slowly. Sor Elena had certainly seen Asher's classroom assessments before selecting her for secondment to the front, and knew where her teachers had recommended self-improvement. "Thank you, Sor," she said, and bowed, as she had always done in the Holiest House at the end of a lesson.

"Goodnight, Asher," answered Sor Elena, and settled herself cross-legged into her meditative pose. Asher put out the fire she had made for herself, and crawled into her tent to sleep.

SHE WAS WOKEN in the middle of the night by screams and clattering metal, and the mules, somewhere in the distance, braying their heads off.

Asher shoved away the pile of blankets and wrappings

and jumped to her feet, pulling her tent up from the ground with her. "What's—"

"We're under attack!" That was Sergeant Barghest—or, no, not Barghest—in the faint light of the stars, Asher could see that the Dedicate who'd spoken had no stripes of command painted on their shoulders. (And never, either, had Asher heard Sergeant Barghest say anything that could possibly be written with an exclamation point.) "Watch out—"

Abruptly the Dedicate launched themself at Asher, shoving her back down to the ground in a tangle of canvas. A streak of light blazed through the spot where she'd been standing. Asher breathed in, twice. That light had been a javelin covered in burning pitch. She could feel bruises blossoming where she'd hit the ground, and where the Dedicate had hit her. "You'd better stay low," rasped the Dedicate, and clambered back to their feet.

Asher shoved her way out of the tent and crouched, squinting through the dark. The mules were gone, who knew where—but Sor Elena sat exactly where Asher had left her last night, still and unmoving.

"The Sor is in command." The Dedicate had rocked back into a watchful stance, eyes forward towards the sky above the battle. "I was called here to guard both of you. She said you weren't to attempt to join the fight. The attackers are heavily armored, and the visibility's bad."

Asher had scored well in armed and unarmed combat training, and her teachers had told her that her night vision was above average. Still, she was seconded to Sor Elena, and she wouldn't question her orders. "Is there anything else I can do to help?"

"No," said Sor Elena. Asher whipped her head round.

The Sor hadn't moved from her position, but her jeweled eyes let out a faint glow. "I can't afford to have my attention split right now. Please remain as you are."

Sor Elena's eyes dimmed again before Asher could respond. She turned to the Dedicate instead. "How many attackers are there? Do you know?"

"The Sor sent me here just as the fighting began," snapped the Dedicate, and then lurched out of the way of another javelin as it went soaring past them. "I don't know a shit-blown thing!"

The profanity in the Dedicate's mouth startled Asher almost as much as the javelin. She had more questions—how and why had the Levastani penetrated so far into Cesteli territory? What was Sor Elena's plan? *Did* Sor Elena have a plan?—but it didn't seem likely the Dedicate could answer any of them. Instead, she focused on Sor Elena. Now that she knew what to look for, she could see that the sister's metal hands were clasped to the command plate in her chest that let her link to the Dedicates. Somewhere out there, Sor Elena's mind was ranging through the battle, leaping from soldier to soldier, taking control of each body for as long as it took to deliver an order or implement an aspect of her strategy before moving onto the next.

The Dedicates were divine vessels, dedicated to the protection of Cesteli State. They were made for this.

In a sense, Sor Elena was made for this too—or rather, had made herself for this. Like many of the sisters who had taken the soul's habit since the war began, she'd designed her form to reflect the knights of old: plates like armor, cuirass and sabatons, protecting the complex clockwork and the godstone core within. Moonlight reflected off the copper scrollwork and embossed ornamentation of her carapace. A shining reflection of her troops, meant to inspire where they caused fear, she might have been a mural painted onto a temple wall—might have been, except that the sisters in the paintings tended to strike martial poses, stances wide, arms high, command plates shining in a way that real godstone never did. They didn't sit quiet and cross-legged on the ground, head bowed, eyes banked, like a statue that had never come to life.

It was the same as when Sor Beatriz had demonstrated the use of the command plate in the classroom. Asher should not have expected it to be different, more dramatic, simply because they were surrounded by the clash of blades and the sound of screams.

She tried to walk herself through the situation as if it were a training exercise, and pretend the smells of overheated metal and spilled blood were happening somewhere else. "Sor Elena must have sent some of the Dedicates to try and take out the javelin launchers." It had been at least a few minutes now since she'd seen any missiles, and the battle-noise had taken on a different tone. "Do you think—"

"I think we'd probably better keep our mouths shut," said the Dedicate, "while those Levastani bastards are targeting us."

Asher swallowed. The Dedicate was probably not frustrated with *her* so much as with the situation. "They must already know the Sor is here, though? Those javelins were—"

As if on cue, another burning javelin came flying through the night.

The Dedicate shouted and flung themself towards Sor Elena. So did Asher. Neither of them were quite fast enough. With a sound like a gasp, Sor Elena's machinery whirred to life—then caught, rattling, on the long piece of metal half-melted through the middle of it.

"Sor!" shrieked Asher, and scrambled on her hands and knees towards Sor Elena. The Dedicate stood in front of her, frozen. The mail on their upper left arm had a soft-edged hole in it where the flaming javelin had gone through it like butter.

Sor Elena reached up an unsteady hand to touch the handle of the javelin that pinned her.

Then, carefully, she lowered her arm again, and turned her head to look at Asher, but it was the Dedicate who spoke.

"Well, Asher—I'm afraid this may be beyond field repair." All trace of the edgy irritability that Asher had heard before in the Dedicate's voice was gone; their voice was full of careful reassurance. *Her* voice, Asher realized, with another small bleak shock—Sor Elena's voice, or at least her words, delivered through the only vessel available. "Still, you won't lack an opportunity to demonstrate your mechanical skills for me. If you can remove the javelin and ensure that any loose parts are removed from the carapace and collected safely for transport, I would be grateful."

Asher swallowed. "Yes—of course, Sor." She sat up on her knees, and looked down at Sor Elena's habit. The metal shook faintly, trapped machinery shrieking in a jangling pattern. The bags that pushed air through Sor Elena's voicepipes wheezed their deflation. Asher wanted to cover her ears.

She reached out towards the javelin, then hesitated. If she pulled the weapon out while Sor Elena was still active, the damage to her internal mechanisms could be even worse, but if she switched her off while they were in the middle of battle—

"Sergeant Barghest's troops have captured the launcher now. The fight will be over soon. It troubles me that the enemy knew where we were." The Dedicate's voice did sound troubled, alarmingly so. The Dedicate's human vocal cords, Asher realized, allowed Sor Elena a greater range of emotion than the pipes of her own habit. "Still, the troops are needed at the front. Asher—there will be less damage to me, and less risk to your hands, if I'm completely inactive while you perform the immediate repairs. Once you've stabilized me as best you're able, you should send some of the Dedicates back with my habit towards the Holiest House in Rouledo. Three should be sufficient for that task. Then you may continue with Sergeant Barghest and the others to the front."

Asher's breath caught. Her lungs felt as skewered as Sor Elena's airbags. "Yes, Sor," she managed to gasp out.

"Once you're there, report to Sor-General Teresa. She'll reassign you and the Dedicates as appropriate." Incredibly, Asher almost thought she could hear a smile in the Dedicate's borrowed voice. "Don't look so nervous. It *is* unfortunate, but you're only a few days from the front. Truly, I expect you'll learn more from this experience than from any training I could provide along the way."

Easy for you to say, Asher caught herself thinking, when you're going back to safety—but that was an absurd thing to think about anyone with a javelin sticking through them. Even a habited sister, who could be damaged, debilitated, or shut down, but not—at least so far as anyone had yet proved—completely killed. Their soul was bound to the metal of their bodies until they chose to release themselves to the heavens.

"One more thing." Sor Elena's arm lifted again—slowly, in painful staccato bursts—until it reached the area on her chest where the command plate sat clamped into a nest of springs and cylinders, godstone to godstone. "Until you reach the front, this is yours."

Asher could barely hear the quiet click of the command plate popping free over the horrible sound of machinery failing. She took it numbly from Sor Elena's hand and attempted to put it in the pocket of her robe. Then she remembered that she was wearing a nightshirt, and placed it awkwardly on the ground instead. The springs of the locking mechanism in Sor Elena's chest still vibrated, raw and exposed, over the cloudy gray of the godstone port. The hollow of dull stone looked like a wound in her bright mail—like a piece had been carved from the flesh that Sor Elena no longer had.

"I'll meet you at the front as soon as I can, Novice Asher," said Sor Elena, through the Dedicate, and switched herself off.

The terrible jerking noise of her impaled innards ground to a stop.

Asher stared over Sor Elena's empty habit at the Dedicate. The Dedicate stared back, then abruptly got to their feet.

"What's your name?" Asher asked them. She'd only said it because she needed to hear them talk—needed the concrete proof, suddenly, that Sor Elena had really left them.

"Svanik," snapped the Dedicate. They turned, upper arms folded, to look in the direction of the fading sounds of battle.

It was impossible to imagine Sor Elena's voice that snappish. Asher turned back towards the empty habit.

Sor Elena would not be able to see how successful Asher was or wasn't in stabilizing her after the injury. Some of Asher's classmates would have been grateful to perform an operation like this unobserved, but Asher knew it was always easier to pass a test when you knew there was somebody watching you do it. Probably that was why they taught you, at the Holiest House, that it was foolish to rely on the presence of anyone but yourself.

But of course, she reminded herself, she *would* have watchers over the next week. She would have the Dedicates.

She thought of their blank identical faces, and felt her shoulders tense up.

Then she bent over Sor Elena to begin the work of carefully removing the javelin.

BARGHEST LOOKED DOWN at Aconite's body. A flaming javelin had lodged straight in their lungs.

Aconite had died because they'd put themself in between the javelin and Barghest. Neither of them had seen the javelin coming. It was the Sor-Commander who had seen it, through the eyes of one of the other Dedicates, and had taken the steps she thought necessary with the tools she had.

Barghest had only realized the danger they'd been in when they heard the thud of Aconite hitting the ground. As they whirled around, Sor Elena had used Aconite to speak to them. "I'm sorry, Sergeant," she'd said. The voice had been ragged, gasping. It did not sound as if Aconite should have been able to speak at all. "I regret this sacrifice, but losing you would be a worse one. And Asher will need you, I think. Please help her as best you can."

Barghest hadn't had time to react then. The fight was still raging, Dedicates and Levastani locked in combat all around them. They'd raised their axe and returned to the work at hand.

Now the battle had drawn to a close. Two other Dedicates were dead, and fifteen Levastani. Given the lack of experience among the unit, they could hardly have done better. Most of these Dedicates had been trained in Alabaca's Holiest House and were only now on their first deployment. Aconite had been one of the few exceptions. They had been assigned here along with one other member of their battalion after a period of recovery from serious injuries. Barghest had valued their experience, and had been looking forward to working with them.

Instead, because Aconite had been standing in a certain place at a certain time, they were dead, and Barghest was alive. It was good to be alive; still, if you were going to owe your life to a dead comrade, you'd rather it was a comrade who'd known what they were doing when they died.

But battle didn't care about a person's preferences.

Barghest straightened. "All right," they said, pitching their voice to carry, "we'll bring Aconite with the others—"

"Sergeant."

Barghest turned. It was Asher, the novice seconded to Sor Elena, with Svanik marching along sullenly behind her. Barghest had only ever seen her standing quiet and composed next to Sor Elena as she reeled off prepared facts from a map. Her novice's robes tended to have very neat folds in them, as if she placed them under a rock each night after taking them off.

Now she was wearing a linen shift. Her curly dark hair was still wild from sleep, and her hands were smeared with grease and ash. "Sergeant, can you recommend me three Dedicates to undertake a separate mission?"

"It depends," Barghest said cautiously, "on what that mission might be, sir."

"Escorting Sor Elena's habit safely back to the Holiest House in Rouledo."

Barghest looked down again at Aconite's body, with a sudden surge of mixed sorrow and relief. Barghest wouldn't have purchased their own life at such a high price, but if the sisters asked sacrifices, they also made their own.

Practically speaking, it made no difference. Barghest knew what their duty was. Still, it helped to be reminded.

"Zechs," they said out loud, "to lead the group. Svelf and Silver seconded." They gave Asher a brisk salute, and thought, privately: No wonder Sor Elena had made sure that Barghest would survive the fight. Asher didn't seem any less competent than other novices Barghest had worked with, but she was as short on field experience as any of the new Dedicates, and command couldn't be taught in the classroom.

Barghest briefly suppressed a mental image of the novice and her wet-behind-the-ears troops, absent any senior leadership, flailing their way across Green Adam's glacial ice like ducklings waddling on a frozen river.

It will be all right, they silently promised the absent Sor Elena. *She'll have my support; I won't let her fail.*

I WATCHED THE novice set her shoulders back, like someone trying to grow a few inches with willpower alone, and thought about how much easier it would have been if she had been felled with the sister.

The sister wasn't even dead, not really. To really get rid of one of those abominations, you had to completely melt them down—and even then, there was the question of souls, or ghosts, or whatever you thought animated the fucking things. The Levastani had melted down hundreds of sisters since the war began, and sent the metal off to the priests for ritual purification afterwards. I heard a rumor that it all eventually got repurposed for drain pipes and trash bins, but that was probably just a joke.

Anyway, nobody had gotten a chance to melt this particular abomination, and so she was going home, safe and sound. The novice, though—she was only human, with ordinary human weaknesses.

If the timing had gone right, I would be on my way home already, command plate in my hand. That had been the plan from the beginning: while the other Levastan troops attacked, I was to use the cover of the confusion to get the command plate away from the sister. Once I was in control of the other Dedicates, all the fighting would stop. The metal sister and her novice really wouldn't have any choice but to surrender.

At that point the sister would most likely have ended up as another set of milk jugs or toasting forks, but as for the novice—well, she was young, and not yet a full abomination, and the Commander might have had sympathy, the way people do for young girls who look like young girls rather than metal monsters; the way nobody had had sympathy for the Dedicate we had ambushed four days ago so that I could take their place on this fun little Cesteli field trip. We had killed that Dedicate, but I think we probably would have taken the novice prisoner or something. I think probably we would have kept her alive.

Only, Commander Martens had gotten the timing wrong. Six days, he'd said, and I'd been counting them, like a prisoner waiting for parole—which I wasn't, of course I wasn't. I'd volunteered for this. All the same, as I lay motionless in a dark tent listening to the faint rattling of a Dedicate across from me breathing in and out, I'd thought: five more days, and then I'm free. Four days. Three. Two days, and then it will all be over, and I'll never have to pretend to be one of these things again.

But the count was still at two days when I woke up in the middle of the night to the sound of battle, without having had a chance to get into position or anything.

Either Martens had made a mistake, or someone had gotten careless and made themself visible, triggered the clash before we were ready. It didn't really matter either way. I'd never get a chance to ask any of them about it now.

"Are you listening?"

I jumped, and realized that this was the second time that the Dedicate sergeant had addressed me. "Apologies, Sergeant, I was just—" The Sergeant waited patiently. I didn't have the next word ready; I hadn't really expected to be given time to finish the excuse. "Um, it's—"

"The first fight is often difficult," said Sergeant Barghest. "There's no shame in that."

Sympathy, from that brainwashed Cesteli puppet, was such a horrible unexpected joke that I very nearly laughed aloud. There was shame in almost everything that had happened last night: shame in the way I'd been unprepared, and shame in the way I'd stumbled around the edges of the battle, doing the bare minimum to defend myself, while Martens' men got slaughtered. If I'd managed to get to the sister in time to save any of them, the sacrifice might have been worth it. But it had all been over too fast, and now I had nothing to show for it except a lot of dead bodies that were supposed to be my backup, and the kindness of someone who didn't know they were my enemy.

"I know," I answered, and braced myself to be set the task of burying the bodies.

I didn't have a face to read, like a real person did, and I was sure that I didn't flinch. Still, they paused, looking at me, and then said, instead, "You should see if you can find where those mules went. If you don't find them by the time the sun's halfway up, come back."

They gave me a nod of dismissal and turned away, presumably to find someone else to bury the bodies, and left me standing there feeling like a rock that had been turned over to show all the worms underneath. I wasn't used to having my emotions seen that way. Back in Levasta I usually had to start shouting before anyone besides my mother remembered that I had emotions at all.

That had been true for Martens and his men, as well. I couldn't say they'd been cruel to me, really, or even rude. I was an abomination as much as any metal Cesteli, but I was their useful abomination, performing a useful task, and that did mean something.

Now all that remained of them was a pile of cleaved limbs and shattered skulls. They weren't quite my first dead bodies; there had been that Dedicate, four days ago. But we'd killed the Dedicate cleanly, flaming javelin puncturing the iron at point-blank range, none of the human flesh underneath exposed. You might have thought the corpse was a statue if it weren't for the smoking hole and the smell of burned meat.

Not that the remains of Martens and his men looked any more human, at this point. At least it was cold enough that there weren't many flies.

I felt my stomach begin to heave as I looked at them, and hastily turned away. Of all the things there were to despise about my particular form of existence—and there were plenty; I had a running list—the fact that nobody had figured out how to get rid of the nausea reflex before they smacked an iron grille over my face was currently right near the top. Perfect soldiers! What a fucking joke! I set my face firmly in the opposite direction, and went trudging off towards the hill, where the mule had been tethered.

The novice was there too, now, packing up her things. She usually kept her hair tied up inside her hood, but today it hung around her face in a disorderly nimbus of frizz, a bit like my mother's. Now that I saw her up close, she actually looked quite a lot like my mother. That didn't mean anything; there were plenty of people with Gedank ancestry on both sides of the war. I steered a wide circle around her, grimly scouring the ground for mule tracks. When I killed her, I would have to do it in a single blow, so that she didn't have time to muster the other Dedicates against me before I took the command plate. I'd never done anything like it before, but that didn't mean it should be difficult. I could easily do it when she was asleep, and as long as I was quiet she'd never wake up, or know what was happening.

"What are you looking for?" said the novice, from my blind spot, and I practically jumped out of my carapace.

"The mules," I answered, without turning. "Sorry. Didn't mean to bother you."

"Oh, no, you didn't—sorry, it's just—if it was something I had," said the novice, "or something I knew about. Sorry. I think the mules ran off that way?"

Did she think I couldn't read a set of tracks? "Great," I said. "Thank you, sir." And I picked up the pace, marching as quickly after the mule tracks as I could without looking like I was flat-out running away from her.

I'd gotten this far. I just had to keep it up for a little longer. Tonight, the novice would go to sleep, and then I could get the unpleasant part over with; then I could go home. After that, Levasta would have a whole unit of other Dedicates to research or use as infiltrators or whatever else would help them win the war faster. They could find another way to use me, after that. I'd never have to do this particular horrible thing again.

But I had to get the unpleasant part over with first.

THE DEDICATE THAT had barreled off to look for the mules came trudging back an hour later, empty-handed. Asher did not believe in omens, which did not stop her from feeling that this was a bad one.

She frowned down at the supplies that the mules had once carried—several panniers of food and her own tent—plus Svanik's personal pack, too bulky for someone with such a significant injury.

"Sergeant," she said, "do you have any suggestions for how to redistribute the weight?"

"I'd recommend a rotation," answered Barghest next to her, "organized by serial number. They can change over at the midday break, and then again tomorrow."

This was all well and good, except that Asher did not know the Dedicates' serial numbers. Self-consciously, she reached into her inner pocket for the command plate. She had not yet figured out a satisfactory method for carrying it safely. On the rare cases that someone other than a habited sister was entrusted with one, best practice recommended a case that mimicked the locking mechanism built over the godstone port in the sisters' habits. However, if Sor Elena had brought a carrying case with her against emergencies, Asher had not been able to locate it, so for right now the inner pocket would have to do.

She squinted at the carved stone disk, reviewed the information engraved on the chips set into it, and then put it carefully away again. "Sergeant," she said, "please tell Cascabela, Aconite, and Titan that—"

"Aconite was killed," said Barghest.

They said it in the same even tone in which they said everything. Asher stared at them. She knew they had lost three Dedicates, but she'd been so busy getting everything ready and trying to think what they would need that she hadn't thought to inquire specifically as to which.

As usual, she was probably imagining the accusing quality in their blank metal stare. Still: "Sergeant," she said, "I'm *sorry*."

"Every battle has losses," Barghest said. And then, even as she opened her mouth to formulate the question, went on: "We also lost Alft and Zekzen. They died as they should have, performing their duty. We remember, and regret, and return to ours."

She wanted to apologize again, but 'we return to ours' seemed fairly clear. "I'll remember, then. Thank you, Barghest."

"It's a very fair way to divide the duties, Commander. I'm sure there won't be any complaints about it, and I'll make sure it's done."

Asher fought back a flush. Was that a reassuring tone in Barghest's voice, or was that just what she wanted to think? "Thank you, Sergeant," she said, and then added, "When we get on the road again, will you walk with me? There's more I'd like to ask you."

Somehow, everything became efficiently organized; somehow, they got on the road. Asher and Barghest walked slightly ahead, with the eight remaining Dedicates marching behind them. The thumping sound of the Dedicates seemed louder and more ominous when she was walking at ground level. She found herself resisting the urge to look behind her to make sure they weren't gaining. She missed her mule.

But, she reminded herself, of all things in this world that a person could not control, it was the absolute purest folly of all to believe that you controlled a mule. All things were temporary. A person adapted. "Sergeant," she said out loud, pitching her voice just loud enough to be heard over the marching of the troops, "I need your help."

Barghest saluted.

"I can learn the names and serial numbers of the Dedicates in the unit." She swore to herself that by tomorrow she would have them memorized. "But I don't know the troops themselves well enough to be able to, uh, reliably distinguish them? If something were to happen—"

It would be easy to let Barghest continue to relay her commands to the appropriate soldiers. It was the same kind of easy as not studying for an exam, or copying someone's homework, and she didn't trust it.

"Yes, of course," Barghest said, and then turned their head to glance at her. "We're designed to make it difficult to identify individuals, Commander."

There it was again—a faintly reassuring tone, unmistakable. She bit her lip at the patronization, even as she felt the tension in her back ease a little. Asher knew her own faults perfectly well: she followed after praise like a poppy to the sun, wilted without it like grass in a drought. Had Barghest picked up on that so quickly?

Still, you had to consider things strategically. Surely any sergeant would rather have an even-tempered, confident commander than one who was crippled by doubt. Especially if that sergeant had concerns about the morale of their troops after a surprise attack and serious losses. Of course Dedicates fought no matter what the circumstances, but thinking about the pains Barghest had already taken to support her and make her look competent in the eyes of the others—it must matter, how they saw her.

So she smiled at Barghest, just as if she really were as confident as they both needed her to be. "Yes, I know, Sergeant. And it wasn't my responsibility before, but it is now. So—I can recognize you, of course." The painted sergeant's stripes on their shoulders were clear enough to see. "And Svanik will be easy now, though—" She put her hand, involuntarily, up to the part of her upper arm that matched the new hole in Svanik's plating. "—um, of course I wish it were for a different reason. What about Cascabela and Titan?"

Titan, she remembered, had taken on their extra pack cheerfully enough. Cascabela had seemed dispirited. But that did not seem enough to pick either of them out, in a group of nine.

"Cascabela came from the same battalion as Aconite," Barghest answered. "Now that Aconite's gone, they're the only one with that death's-head on their wrist." They pointed to a spot on their lower left arm. There was a small dragon sketched out there in flaked green paint that she'd never noticed before.

It looked like the kind of tattoo her older brother had gotten when he wanted to scandalize her parents. She raised her eyebrows at Barghest.

"You won't see any others like mine among the troops," said Barghest, misinterpreting her question. Asher found it something of a relief. They didn't actually have an uncanny ability to read her mind, it was just that up until now she'd been predictable. "My battalion graduated years ago. Those of us who survive are mostly officers by now, and we're all scattered across the front. Aconite and Cascabela were lucky to stay together as long as they did."

"The death's-head—is that something to do with the fact that they're both named for poisonous plants?"

"Each trainer has their own system of naming their troops. Many battalions will make some kind of symbol out of that, if they can. Not all, of course. You won't see anything on the wrists of Svanik, or any of the other rookies from Rouledo—that's Tvell, Dreizen, and Firzen."

Tvell, Dreizen, Firzen, Svanik—"Oh, *no*," said Asher, as she put it together for the first time. "It's just numbers, isn't it? But in Karyozi, so you don't notice." The number-words in Karyozi were close enough to the ones in grandfather's native Gedank tongue that she felt a little embarrassed for not making the connection.

"I'm told that each year their trainer uses a different

language. But it's difficult to make a meaningful symbol from that."

"Yes, I can imagine," Asher said, ruefully. "So I'll have to find some other way to distinguish Tvell, Dreizen, and Firzen?"

"Titan doesn't have a battalion mark either, but they've got a welded patch on their upper right arm, a little above where mine is. For the rest, it's easy enough to tell, once you get to know their personalities."

Asher once again resisted the urge to look behind her as she contemplated the daunting prospect of distinguishing Dedicates by personality. If she hadn't met Svanik, she wouldn't have thought it possible. Maybe if someone else had been the Sergeant, rather than calm, strait-laced Barghest, she'd be more used to the idea of Dedicates that talked and bickered like ordinary people. But she felt guilty as soon as that thought crossed her mind; surely no one could have helped her more last night and this morning than Barghest, bland or no.

They had been walking some time now on an upward slope, Green Adam looming ever-larger on the left, and Asher was starting to feel the effort in her calves and back. The black dirt of the path beneath their feet crunched with frost. The bright noon sun struck blue lights off the encroaching ice and the battered metal of Barghest's carapace. Asher fumbled in the pocket of her robe for her tinted glasses, and put them on. The world blessedly dimmed, and so did Barghest.

It occurred to Asher to ask, "Your eyes—"

"We have resin visors inside we can lower as we choose," said Barghest, "but it's good of you to think of it."

Asher sighed. "I wish I had a diagram of how you're made, so I knew what to worry about."

"Firzen likely has one," offered Barghest. "They're medic-trained. I'll ask them for you."

"No, I should," said Asher, without enthusiasm. If you set out to learn something, you had to test yourself somehow. "I'll see if I can pick them out of the crowd this evening."

There was a slight pause. Barghest said, "It's the sergeant's responsibility to interface between their commander and the troops."

Asher looked over at them, but their head was turned straight forward. There was nothing about their body language she could read. She needed to get much better at this. "Are you saying I *shouldn't* ask Firzen myself, or that I don't have to?"

"I wouldn't say what you should or shouldn't do, Commander. That it's not necessary is all that I meant."

Sor Elena hadn't, it was true. But Sor Elena also had seemed to follow along with Barghest's reports without difficulty, and had needed no help to know which of her troops was which. She opened her mouth to say this, but Green Adam spoke first. An enormous rumbling came from below them. The frozen ground trembled and the sky to the west abruptly darkened. As the light changed, Asher's vision dimmed through her glasses, and, thinking of the Dedicates and their visors, she threw up her arm as she'd seen Sor Elena do to call a halt.

They stood for a minute, Asher's hand raised up to her goggles, ready to take them off—but the sky lightened quickly enough, the cloud that had belched up dissipating in the cold breeze, and the ground settled back into stillness. Asher breathed out.

"Was that—"

For the first time, Asher heard something like

discomfort in Barghest's voice, and answered quickly to reassure them. "No—it's not the volcano, just one of the geysers. Not all of them send up water. Sometimes it's steam or smoke."

Barghest grunted an acknowledgment and shouldered their pack back into position. Then they looked to her—waiting, she realized, for a signal to resume the march.

Asher put up her arm again, high as she could, and gestured forward with it. Then she started walking without looking behind her. It felt absurd that simply by making a silly gesture she could set nine fully-armed Dedicates into motion, but as she walked, she heard the regular thumping pick up again behind her, and knew that they were following.

I DIDN'T LIKE how the ground shook while we were walking. We saw a geyser, too, and I was glad that I wasn't the only one who startled at the sudden jet of water. I hadn't experienced Cesteli's aggressive geography since I was little. It was enough to make you wonder why anyone would want to conquer a place like this—and admittedly, when the religious freaks of Cesteli first declared their independence, the Levastan Emperor at the time had apparently said something along the lines of 'good riddance.' It had taken Levasta four hundred years or so to decide they might want this unstable little patch of land back, on the pretext that they had a responsibility towards their ancestral territory and they disapproved of what the Cesteli were doing with it.

I was only Levastani by circumstance, and I didn't have any particularly strong feelings about Levasta's historical borders. However, I did have strong personal reasons to disapprove of Cesteli State, so here I was, back on shaky ground.

I couldn't say I was enjoying it.

The other Dedicates didn't like it either—not the landscape, nor how slowly we were crossing it. I heard mutterings around me, and, after a while, the Sergeant fell back from where they'd been walking ahead with the novice. They said a word to each member of the unit in turn, and, one by one, I saw backs and shoulders straighten. It was sort of fascinating to watch. I'd seen human commanders with that gift before, but I hadn't thought the sisters would let it flourish in one of their puppets.

Eventually, they came to me. "You're holding up well," they said.

After this morning's near-misses, I'd been trying not to let anything show at all, but maybe that was a mistake. I said, "I'll be glad when we get off this mountain, sir."

Barghest nodded, then pitched their voice a little quieter. "Last night—during the battle, I noticed you seemed to have a little difficulty with the range of motion of your lower arms."

I felt my face warm under its metal. "Sergeant, I—"

When it became clear I wasn't going to finish the sentence, Barghest said politely, "If you're willing, I would be glad to practice with you in the evenings. It seems we'll be longer on the road than expected. We may as well turn the time to some use."

I looked at Barghest, and wondered what my mother would say about the ethics of accepting a gift from a person if you meant to use it to hurt them later. Bad ethics, probably. It was the kind of thing that set a bad example for the gods—at least, if you were Gedank, and believed that your gods could be taught. But Barghest wasn't a person, really. Even coming to offer me training wasn't a real choice they had made. It was just part of their duty, imposed on them by their Sor-Commanders and their distant Cesteli gods, to make sure I was the most efficient killing machine I could be.

"I would really appreciate that, Sergeant," I said, and bowed my head. "I know I have a lot to learn."

"It isn't any trouble." I thought I heard something like a smile in Barghest's voice. "Honing skills with a comrade is a pleasure. It would do me good, too."

"I would think you'd get plenty of practice in, just on the field," I said.

"That's duty," said Barghest, "not pleasure. For me, at least." Their tone was mild. "Though some do take joy in their duty, and there's no shame in that."

After a moment, I said, "No, I like sparring better than battle, too."

Barghest nodded, unsurprised. They thought I was soft, probably, and needed the encouragement. If they'd seen me halfheartedly fending off javelins yesterday, they must have seen, too, that I hadn't killed anybody in that fight.

They gave me a clap on the shoulder with their upper right arm, and continued on down the line.

I'd seen them kill at least three people yesterday, and given how distracted I'd been, the number was probably much higher than that. So you couldn't say it mattered much whether they thought it was fun or not.

The ground shook again right as the sun started to go down. As everyone wobbled and steadied themselves against the side of the mountain, the novice called another halt. When she took off her dark glasses, her eyes peered down at us anxiously. She didn't seem to be enjoying her experience of command.

The knowledge that I planned to kill her tonight crashed down on me abruptly, as it had been doing intermittently all throughout the course of the day. Every time my stomach started to churn again, which was frankly fucking ridiculous. Nothing like this had happened when we ambushed that Dedicate four days ago. I hadn't thought about that at all beforehand except as a task to be gotten through, and seeing their corpse with the javelin through it hadn't made me feel sick at all. Of course I'd thought about it afterwards—the first few times someone called me by the name of the Dedicate we'd killed, until I got used to it—but in a blank sort of way. I didn't *feel* things about it.

Well, I didn't feel anything about killing the novice either, really. It was just a physiological reaction; I'd seen some real dead bodies now, and the parts of my system that were still human hadn't liked it, and didn't want to see more. But I would cope.

In the meantime, I had to somehow get through all the usual tasks of making camp. More of them than usual, actually, since Alft, my assigned tentmate, had died in yesterday's battle. In a way that was a blessing. I wouldn't have to worry about waking them when I got up tonight. On the other hand, the tent was a different model than the one we used in the Levastan army, and on the previous nights I'd been leaving most of the setup work to Alft.

Alft had never complained. I'd assumed this was normal until a day or two after I got there, when I happened to be paying attention as two of the others— Svanik and Zekzen, I think—attempted to set up their tent. After hearing them swear at each other, I'd found myself reluctantly grateful for Alft.

Now I swore at myself, as the tent fell down on my head for the second time. When I struggled out from under the cloth, Barghest called out to me over the noise of the camp. "Help me set up Svanik's, and then we'll do yours."

Svanik clutched their armful of poles defensively. "I don't need help."

"That's as may be, but I want Firzen to take a look at your arm while there's still light. That's an order, Svanik."

Svanik muttered their way over to Firzen. I shuffled towards Barghest, not much more gracefully. I'd made it halfway across the camp when everything around me went hushed.

When I looked over, I saw the novice was coming down among us.

She was heading towards Firzen and Svanik, but her path would take her right past me. Not that it mattered right now—even if I could kill her quickly enough, I wouldn't be able to grab the plate before the others were on me. And Barghest was heading in our direction now, too.

My stomach was starting to roil again. She and the sister had always stayed separate, above us. Couldn't she hear, by the silence, how her presence disturbed the whole camp? Didn't she know this wasn't her place? Looking at her, I could see exactly where I'd twist her neck off her shoulders, the same way Barghest had twisted Martens' yesterday; I could hear in my mind how it would sound. I wished, desperately, that someone else would make some other kind of noise.

My mother always taught me that you have to be

careful with wishes. Sometimes our gods think it's funny to treat them as prayers.

The sound rang into the silence like an explosive. I had a moment of horrified self-disgust at the way my legs were shaking before I realized that the whole world had gone unsteady, and the ground next to the novice was falling away. The novice was staring at it too. Her face was round and shocked. Somewhere, Barghest was shouting. I saw the novice's mouth open; I saw her feet starting to slip.

Instinctively, I reached out a hand to pull her towards me to safety—

What was I, a fucking idiot? I could take the plate later from her corpse. As snow and rock from up the mountain rained down around us, I jerked myself backwards onto solid ground and let her fall.

ASHER BECAME AWARE, first, that she hurt everywhere, and second, that she was cold. She opened her eyes and saw a wall of sheared-off snowy rock, jagged like a carelessly pleated ruff; above that, ice; above that, the peak of Green Adam, farther and higher by far than she knew it ought to be. She'd never been one for vertigo, but the disorientation of this discovery nearly made her dizzy.

Either that, or she was just concussed.

Behind her there were voices, arguing.

"—careless and shameful. She could have died!"

"Sir, she was already falling. I tried, but I couldn't—"

"She's awake!" said another voice much closer, and when she opened her eyes again, she saw a Dedicate in front of her, peering down. The Dedicate's carapace had at least six visible dents in it. *Barghest*, she thought, and then blinked and looked again. This Dedicate had no sergeant's stripes painted on their shoulders, and no emblem on their wrist. So the dents must be new, from their tumble down into this canyon, and if they'd been sent to watch over her, this must be—she tried desperately to remember the names on the plate.

"Firzen?" she guessed. At least if she'd gotten it wrong, she could blame the hypothetical concussion.

"Yes? Yes, that's right." Firzen sounded unflatteringly shocked.

A second Dedicate came to join Firzen in Asher's field of vision. Red stripes on their shoulders: Barghest, without any doubt. "Glad to see you're awake, Commander," they said, so calmly that she almost wondered if she'd imagined the conversation before.

She coughed, and pushed herself up carefully into a sitting position. Her ribs twinged but didn't feel broken. The last thing she remembered was walking towards a group of Dedicates, trying to remember which one was Firzen. She searched desperately in her head for appropriate-sounding words. "Status report, Sergeant?"

"There seems to have been something of a topographical disturbance, Commander," Barghest answered. From the back, someone snorted. "Unfortunately, our previous path is unusable." They paused a moment before adding, "We were concerned for your life."

"It's all right." Asher shrugged to demonstrate how alive she was, and regretted it immediately. "The troops?"

"The others climbed down to join us once it became clear the way forward was impassable. Cascabela has lost functionality in both of their right arms and Dreizen will be walking with a limp until we can get them better care, but both of them should be able to complete a march.

Titan and Firzen have taken only cosmetic damage. Svanik didn't injure any limbs, but Firzen is concerned that there may be complications from their prior injury." Barghest paused a moment, then went on: "Unfortunately, we haven't located Tvell, Dirk, or Baselard."

Asher closed her eyes, took a breath, and opened them again. 'Climbed down to join *us*,' Barghest had said. "And what's your condition, Sergeant?"

"Functional," answered Barghest.

Asher thought she saw Firzen twitch slightly. All the more reason to try to talk to Firzen later. Hopefully they still had their book or whatever medical diagrams they'd brought—

Which reminded her of another question. "What supplies do we have? Any?"

"No tents. One or two packs came down with us, but the food won't last long, with seven. Tvell was near the supplies when the quake hit, so it's possible they were able to salvage more, if we can locate them."

"Has anyone lit a fire yet to signal them? *Can* we light a fire?"

"We can," said Barghest, neutrally, and moved their upper right hand to their lower left arm. A small compartment in the side of the arm flipped open, from which Barghest withdrew a small tinderbox. "Is that your order, sir?"

"Yes—no, wait." It was hard to think, through her dizziness and aching head, but if Barghest hadn't decided on their own to start a fire yet, there must surely be a reason.

"Sir," said one of the Dedicates behind her, "could you use the control plate?"

"Titan," said Barghest. Asher wasn't sure whether that

was a rebuke for the Dedicate who'd spoken out of turn, or simply an attempt to support her ongoing efforts to learn which Dedicate was which. Either way, struggling around to look at Titan gave her time to reconsider. They'd come under attack by the Levastani less than a day's travel away from here. The only silver lining to the disaster that they'd stumbled into was the fact that enemy soldiers would have a harder time finding them in the changed landscape—unless they lit a signal fire and led the enemy straight to them.

Barghest knew that, and Titan probably did too.

"You're absolutely right," she told them. "Thank you for the reminder."

"You're welcome, Commander!" said Titan, brightly.

It sounded sarcastic, but maybe that was just because she couldn't possibly imagine anybody being cheerful under these circumstances.

Asher shifted to fumble her hand into her pocket, noticing in some dismay as she did that her plain wool robe had a whole catalog of new holes and slashes from her fall. As her fingers closed around the rim of the plate, she felt a sudden panic in case it had broken. She'd never heard of this happening by accident; a broken plate was a last-stand kind of event, when all the Dedicates protecting a sister were dead, and all other hope of keeping the technology out of enemy hands was lost. But she'd never heard of a plate tumbling down a cliff in someone's pocket through an avalanche either.

Fortunately, the flat stone circle of the plate looked completely whole as she drew it out. It felt heavier than it looked. Godstone was denser than most common rock, though curiously easy to melt and shape. Raw godstone, untreated, channeled memories and impressions from the souls of those who had touched it; the first humans to interact with it had thought they were being sent visions, long before scientific soteriologists began to research practical applications for its use. Cesteli theologians theorized that the material was what remained of the earliest mortals who'd become worthy of ascending to godhood, and built the road to the heavens.

She turned the plate over in her hands, searching anxiously for new cracks or damage, but saw only the usual triangular divots that held the Dedicates' chips. Each irreplaceable chip, neatly engraved with the Dedicates' serial number, was half of a sympathetic pair. The other half was plated to the base of the Dedicate's skull: a direct resonance with their soul.

Only the highest-ranked military sisters, members of the High Command, knew how to release a chip from one command plate. Otherwise, they were supposed to be locked in place. Asher took the time to count them anyway, her thumb brushing each one: Cascabela, Titan, Firzen, Dreizen, Svanik, who were here; Tvell, Dirk, Baselard, who were lost; Zechs, Svelf, Silver, who had left with Sor Elena's habit; Aconite, Alft, Zekzen, who were dead. And Barghest, the only one with a splash of color, red dot for a sergeant.

Asher had not yet completed her training with the command plate. Her spirit had never been anywhere before other than the inside of her own body. Still, she knew the basic principles: godstone resonated with itself, and with human skin and bone, to serve as a conduit for the soul. She breathed in and placed her thumb down hard on Dirk's chip.

At first, the feeling was almost enjoyable—like the floaty feeling one got towards the end of a fast day, after the hunger had passed, dreamy and tinged with the uneasy knowledge that this pleasant sensation meant the body was starved for resources. Then, all at once, it was no longer pleasant at all. She was in her body and elsewhere, she was stretched at every point, she was bound in two places by tenuous, straining threads—

She could see nothing, until she opened a pair of eyes that were not her own. Then she was looking at Barghest, and she was also looking at a snowy world divided into thin partitions by a metal grille.

"Dirk," she tried to say, and realized too late from the way Firzen and Titan suddenly turned to her that she'd said it with her own mouth and not Dirk's. She could feel the straining breaths Dirk took, labored and too far apart.

Through the grille, she saw a helmet and an arm belonging to a body that lay under a pile of ice. The arm had an emblem painted on the wrist: a dagger. Baselard.

Asher breathed with Dirk's lungs, in and out, and with her own. Seized with a sudden panic that she'd somehow forget to operate one set or the other, she pulled her thumb away. The threads that held her to her body snapped back, almost painfully, and she gasped.

The Dedicates hovered around her. She thought about Barghest's expressionless list of the dead after the last battle, and felt a sudden reluctance to be the bearer of more bad news, but this was a commander's duty and there was no use in thinking she could avoid it. "Dirk is wounded," she said, out loud. "They're unconscious, I think. I—I think—"

She looked down at Baselard's chip. She should put her thumb on it and confirm, but inhabiting Dirk's damaged body had been terrifying enough.

"—I think Baselard is dead."

She was a coward, but she wasn't ready to know what it was like to have her spirit try and connect to a dead Dedicate.

Barghest nodded, slowly, and Firzen looked away.

Asher took a deep breath. It was the last thing she wanted to do, but: "I'm going to try Tvell," she said, and moved her thumb to Tvell's chip.

Tvell was alive, and awake. She knew it as soon as the threads of her consciousness snagged onto them; there was an odd, distinct sensation of overlay, something between the feeling of self-as-other that one sometimes got in dreams and the sensation of shoving someone else physically aside to make room. They were standing on functional legs, looking out over a cliffside. She was so glad that she would not have to report back another death that she could have cried.

"Tvell," she said out loud—it came out of the right mouth, this time, echoing in the silence of the mountain—and turned to try and survey the landscape. Immediately she realized that this was a mistake, as her foot slipped and her stomach hitched in panic. Hastily, she pressed Tvell's body flat back against the wall of the mountain behind her. The ledge of ice on which they stood was *very* narrow. "Where are you?"

Sir—the voice seemed to come at the bottom of her own throat, and she very nearly jumped in both Tvell's body and her own—*I'm not too far from where we were before. The part of the path I was standing on didn't fall. I can make my way along it, if I'm* very careful.

There was a definite edge on the last two words. Asher swallowed, with her own throat, and closed her eyes in her own body, and answered, in Tvell's voice: "Good? Good! Well done."

Her own intonations in Tvell's hollow tenor rang very strangely in her own ears. It seemed silly, besides, to have to communicate with Tvell by puppeteering them. A commander must have a way to give orders without broadcasting their plans to everybody around. She tried subvocalizing, formulating words in the back of her throat without speaking. *Ah—we fell into the ravine somewhere around there, I think?* In Tvell's body, she looked down at the great gash in the landscape below her feet; in her own, she looked up. From neither set of eyes could she see the other—at least not without leaning Tvell's heavy body forward, which she wasn't going to do without a much better sense of how to safely balance it. *All the others are with me, except for Dirk and Baselard.*

They were right in front of me. I think they fell further down the mountain. Should I look for them, sir?

She tried to think, first, about tactics. Even if Dirk could be saved, even if Tvell could find them, would it be possible for Tvell to carry the body of another Dedicate all the way to safety by themself, along this narrow ledge? The ridge had supported Tvell's weight so far, but two Dedicates might well be too much for it.

Then she remembered the weight of Dirk's eyelids, as she opened them; the feel of their lungs, raggedly breathing in and out.

*If you can search safely—*She closed both sets of eyes and tried to visualize the map she'd studied just the day before. The path they'd been taking switched back and forth along the mountain as it descended. *I think Dirk is below you, but not so far that you shouldn't see them when the path bends. If you think you can help them without endangering yourself—but I don't want to lose two in trying to help one?*

44

There was a small pause, and Asher realized that she had said Dirk, had said *one*—so Tvell, too, now must know that Baselard was dead. But the only answer they gave was, *Understood.*

Asher swallowed, with Tvell's throat. *Our paths should reconnect—it would normally be two days' walk, but our progress may be slow, and we don't know how the earthquake will have changed the landscape. Don't worry about making time. Just keep forward, and be careful? Don't walk on any piece of ice without testing your weight on it first.*

Yes, sir, answered Tvell, and again she thought she caught a hint of sharpness. She supposed that was fair. After all, she was the one who had almost lost them their balance.

Still, there were areas of the mountain they'd need to avoid—she thought with a certain panic of the web of underground springs, the geysers, the elevation charts and points of instability that she had so carefully studied. She couldn't convey all that information to Tvell right now, and she couldn't stay with them to guide them either, not with the rest of the Dedicates waiting for her. Sor Elena or another trained sister could have been effectively in both places at once, but it was taking all Asher's concentration just to avoid moving any of Tvell's limbs in a way that would destabilize them.

She wished Tvell had a way to initiate connection with her, that their contact didn't go just the one way. *I'll check in with you every six hours,* she told them. *If you run into an obstacle you can't surmount, don't try to push past or detour. Stay where you are, and wait for my orders. I promise I'll be back with you soon.*

Yes, sir.

Asher removed her thumb from the chip, and opened her own eyes, slightly startled now to find them wet with relief.

"Tvell's alive."

Because she was watching for it, she saw Barghest and Firzen's shoulders both relax. "You were quiet a long time," said Firzen, almost accusingly.

Asher bit back the urge to offer up an excuse. She wanted to give Firzen a reason that they could sympathize with and understand—but for right now she was their commander, and they needed to believe in her competence more than they needed to like her.

Maybe she was getting wiser, or maybe it was just the thought of Barghest's disapproval if she didn't do her best to act like a proper commander. Either way, she was grateful for it. "I told Tvell to continue making their way northwards?" she said, heard the questioning tone in her voice, and went on, louder: "We should do the same. If we make reasonable time, we can rendezvous with them at the base of Green Adam, on the road towards Fort Videyo."

"How will we get there?" asked one of the Dedicates behind her. "We're off the path, and we lost the map!"

Asher attempted to push herself to her feet. This turned out to be a bad idea. It felt like she had to force every muscle to work individually. Her body screamed pain at her in a way that Tvell's absolutely had not. Barghest stepped forward immediately to offer an arm; she used it to leverage herself the rest of the way up and gave the rest of the Dedicates—her unit, her soldiers—the most confident attempt at a smile she could muster up.

Her unit, her soldiers, looked back at her blankly. Cascabela's arms were crossed, and Titan tipped their

46

head in a response that she couldn't help but read as dubious. But Barghest was a comforting presence at her back, and she knew, she thought, what they needed from her.

"Don't worry," she told them. "I've studied the map—it's up here." And she brought her hand up to her head. "I promise you, I'll get us safe through."

ASHER SAID SHE could walk unaided. Barghest was in no position to contradict her, so they took the rear guard and watched the remains of their unit picking their way carefully over crumbling snow.

There were too few of them, and none of them moving as well as they should, except Titan and Firzen—and Firzen had slowed their pace to match Svanik's, who was, in turn, doing their grim best to pretend that Firzen wasn't there. Cascabela made good enough time, but grunted in pain every time one of their injured arms banged against the cliffside; Dreizen was trying to go too fast on their bad leg.

Aside from the shuffling crunch of metal on snow and rock, they walked in uncharacteristic silence. It was Dreizen who eventually broke it. They slipped on a patch of ice, windmilled all four of their arms to stop themself falling, then let out a short, winded laugh: "Should have had skates!"

Svanik huffed a response: "Never again."

This was clearly an old joke between them. Dreizen laughed again, louder, and Firzen joined in. Barghest visualized the sound bouncing off the snow and reverberating through the mountain like exploding cannon fire. Wearily, they said, "Low voices, please."

"Laughing our way to another avalanche," said Titan, softly.

"Noise doesn't cause avalanches," said Asher.

Barghest turned their attention towards Asher toiling along at the front, and so did the others—especially Firzen and Dreizen, who had clearly forgotten she was close enough to hear their chatter. She looked over her shoulder, eyes invisible behind her snow-glasses, and added, "I thought it might be helpful to know that noise doesn't make the snow fall? That's a myth. It's usually just something to do with the weather—too much wind, or sun. Um."

"Thank you," said Barghest, and tried to figure out how to remind their commander that, regardless of the causes of avalanches, a loud noise could easily bring more Levastan soldiers down on their heads.

"So we could get another one no matter what we do?" asked Firzen, somewhat anxiously.

"Control," snarled Cascabela, "is an illusion."

It was the first thing Cascabela had said all day. In fact, Barghest realized, this was the first time they'd heard Cascabela speak since the Levastan attack.

It did hit people like this, sometimes. Cascabela was no raw recruit, but they had been close with Aconite—they had managed to stay together with Aconite, somehow, through all their years in the field—and there was a difference between witnessing a comrade's death, and losing the last person you had.

Under normal circumstances, Barghest would have noticed earlier. They would have made time to go talk to Cascabela last night and give them the space to speak of their grief.

The current circumstances were very far from normal.

All the same, Barghest put 'talk to Cascabela about Aconite' back near the top of their list of tasks to be done when they made camp, right below 'talk with Firzen about Svanik's injuries' and 'talk to Asher about the possibility of running into Levastan patrols,' and above the self-indulgent pleasure of 'set up a sparring match.'

Nobody had warned them, when they made sergeant two years ago, that the position involved so much talking.

Nobody had warned them, either, that being in charge meant nobody came to check in on you, when you found yourself in a situation you didn't have enough answers for; when your fellows were gone, and your heart hurt, and you were weary; when somebody's friend had died to keep you alive, and you had to find something to say to them that didn't have any of your own feelings in it. You watched out for their well-being, when you were the sergeant. They didn't watch out for yours.

There were the sisters, of course. A long time ago, one could perhaps have expected to find comfort there. But the sisters were not anymore in the business of solace these days—at least, not the ones who went to war. The Dedicates were not their children, but their soldiers. If Barghest wanted a superior officer to take responsibility for their emotional well-being, they should have turned down their promotion—and if they hadn't been promoted, they might well have been the one sacrificed to protect some other superior officer.

You couldn't know. You only did your job. Barghest looked ahead at Asher, but she was facing forward again, and all they could see was her back. Without the weight of her pack to disguise it, it looked smaller and more fragile than ever before. There was nothing reassuring in those hunched shoulders, no sense that the burden of command could be safely displaced.

The undyed wool of her dark gray cloak was lightly flecked with white. It had begun to snow again.

There was no purpose in thoughts like these. Morale was the thing. Morale, and (quiet) conversation. "Commander," Barghest said.

Asher put a hand up against the canyon wall to balance herself, and looked backwards. "Yes?"

"What are some other myths about this kind of territory? Things we might believe, without knowing they're false?"

"Oh," said Asher. "Um, well—" Her face curved, the way those of unaltered humans sometimes did to indicate happiness or hopefulness or nerves. "Have you heard the one about spitting, if you're buried in snow, to know which way is up?"

"About *what*," said Titan.

"They made sure to tell us that one was false. But I've never heard of anyone who actually believed it was true. I think you'd have to be pretty gullible?"

Dreizen laughed. It was louder than Barghest would have liked, but not really that much louder than the sound of six injured Dedicates crunching their way through packed snow. Barghest thought about it, and decided the benefit was likely greater than the cost.

It warmed her, for a little, hearing the laughter behind her. She couldn't take much credit for it—Barghest, once again, had tossed her the lead—but she hadn't fumbled it, and that felt like an achievement in itself.

It was the same glow of pride she'd always gotten

from making her fellow students laugh over lunch at the Holiest House; not that she'd managed it more or less often than anybody else, but she'd always felt that she had to work harder than other people to achieve the effect, which made it mean more.

This wasn't *so* different from keeping the conversation spinning over pea soup or soft yogurt. And though of course it mattered that she was the commander—well, she'd been ahead of many of her peers academically, and they'd forgiven her for it. She had managed that. She could manage this.

And she could, for a while—but as the snow fell harder and her body got colder, conversation dried up behind her, and she couldn't think of any way to get it started again. After a while, she couldn't even remember why it had seemed important to try. Probably her Dedicates were all working as hard as she was simply to put one foot in front of the other. Perhaps they, too, were having the same difficulties with staying present in the moment, rather than floating away, over the canyon and up towards Tvell or Dirk—

She felt a warm grip close round her elbow. "Commander." Barghest was barely visible through the drifting white, but it could be nobody else.

Asher admitted defeat. "Yes."

She turned around and heaved the protesting muscles of her arms up high, making herself as visible as she could in the hard-blowing snow. "Let's explore the area? We'll see if we can find an overhang, or—or something."

"Yes, sir!"

The response came in a ragged chorus, the number of voices impossible to distinguish. Asher wiped off her snow-glasses, then pushed them up on her forehead, trying to squint through the swirling white. Icy wind slammed immediately into her eyes. "Troops! Sound off!"

"Barghest," said Barghest, dutifully, although they were standing right next to her, and Asher felt a sudden rush of affection for them.

"Dreizen!"

"Titan."

"Cascabela."

"Firzen." A beat. "And Svanik."

Surely those answers had come in the same deep tenor. "Firzen?" Asher called. "You're with Svanik?"

"I'm here," snapped another voice—light and exhausted, unmistakably Svanik's—and Asher's shoulders relaxed a little.

"All right. Svanik and—" Which was the one with the crunched right arms? She ran through Barghest's list in her head, then remembered the crumpled death's-head on the battered metal wrist. "—and Cascabela, come up here and wait with me while the others look? We'll— we'll be the base so no one else gets lost."

It was a paper-thin excuse to salve the pride of the injured Dedicates—and her own—but no one challenged her. Svanik and Cascabela trudged over. Asher stood in between them, huddling into her cloak, and resisted the impulse to edge closer to the faint warmth that Svanik generated. Cascabela didn't seem to be giving off quite as much heat. Perhaps it was because of the damage to their artificial arm. She really needed to look at that diagram of Firzen's, if Firzen still had it, if they were ever somewhere dry...

She'd felt warmer when she was walking. Standing, it was hard to think of anything but the cold, and the bruised, muscle-deep aches all through her body. Her joints felt like they were locking in place. Neither Svanik nor Cascabela seemed inclined to talk, which might have served as a distraction. Her gloved hand delved into her pocket and wrapped around the command plate. She should drift over to Dirk and Tvell—she'd promised to check in every six hours, and it must have been nearly that long—but instinctively she felt it dangerous. If your spirit left your body at a moment like this, how could you ever convince it to return?

"Commander!"

Asher jumped to attention once more, as one of the Dedicates, unidentifiable in the swirling white, came back towards them. "Sir, we found a cave!"

Asher sucked in a breath, then found she couldn't summon the energy for words and simply followed the looming silhouette across to the other side of the canyon. Several feet ahead of them, she could just barely see a break in the bulk of the rock.

The promise of shelter propelled her forward. From further in the cave, a light flamed in the metal palm of another Dedicate, illuminating the dark grille of their face. "We've got tinder," they remarked, "but nothing to start a proper fire with, so we'd better get ourselves arranged quickly if we don't want to be tripping over each other like the holy fools in a mystery play."

Everything got rather loud rather fast, as the Dedicates lowered themselves to the ground, clanking against the rock and the stalactites and each other. The cave seemed far too small, and Asher backed herself up against the wall to give them all more room. She knew, in a fuzzy sort of way, that she ought to be contributing somehow, but all she seemed to be able to do was wrap her arms around herself and shiver. With so many Dedicates crammed in together, the temperature in the cave was beginning to rise, but she still felt cold to her core. The snow on her sodden cloak was melting into slush.

"Hey! Hey—Commander!"

For the third time, the sound of her title summoned Asher back to herself. She hauled her eyes open and stared at the dark silhouette crouching in front of her, a match cupped in their lower left hand.

"You're going to freeze like this," rumbled the Dedicate, "and then you'll be *completely* useless." They held out another hand, their upper right—one of the ones that had flesh and blood in there somewhere, though you wouldn't know it to look at it. "Better stay next to me, all right?"

Like a person in a dream, Asher reached out and took the hand that was offered. Despite the lingering damp from the snow, the iron felt warm as a sun-baked stone.

"There you go," said the Dedicate, kindly, and patted her shoulder with one of their other hands.

Asher groped for a response. Surely, she thought foggily, this couldn't be appropriate for a commanding officer. There was fraternization, and then there was using your troops as portable hand-warmers. Sor Elena would never have done it.

But she was so cold, except where she held the Dedicate's hand; the faint whirring of their machinery promised heat as much as the crackling of the fire, and unlike those she traveled with—unlike Sor Elena—she was only human.

She nodded wearily at the Dedicate, and said, "Thank you."

*　　*　　*

OF COURSE I hadn't wanted to offer. I'd waited for what seemed like forever, but nobody else had seemed to notice the thousand-yard stare on the battered face of the novice, the way she huddled into her frozen cloak with nothing to keep her warm. The thought had even crossed my mind that it might be deliberate, a kind of passive resistance— maybe they were all hoping she'd freeze to death and leave them alone—but Barghest wasn't doing anything either, and I knew for a fact now what lengths they would go to in order to keep her alive. Poor Barghest.

And poor me, too—because over the long cold slog of the day, I'd come to the depressing conclusion that it was perhaps for the best that Barghest had stopped her dying in that fall. I *should* have pulled her back from the brink; I would have, if I'd had time to think it through. In all the chaos of the earthquake, I could have taken the command plate from her easily, then made her guide us down.

I should have known better. When it seemed like the gods had done your work for you, it was almost always a trap.

Now the maps were lost, and nobody else seemed to know the way off the altered landscape of the mountain. Over the course of that long cold afternoon I'd had plenty of time to contemplate exactly how much good it would do me to take the command plate from her corpse, just to keep us all going in circles until we starved to death.

And besides—she'd looked so *unbelievably* pathetic.

Now she was curled in a kind of cocoon in front of me, her head resting awkwardly on one of my left arms and the two right ones braced carefully over her, and I kept thinking how much the gods would laugh if I rolled over in my sleep or something and accidentally squashed her anyway. Unaltered humans were horribly easy to injure.

I'd once accidentally broken two of my mother's ribs, and, unlike the novice, she hadn't just fallen off a cliff at the time.

Her lungs rasped as the air came in and out of them—from all the shouting she'd been doing to keep us talking, or from a burgeoning cold, or both—and because she was right under my nose, the noise stood out even among the small symphony of whirs, rumbles and snores from the other Dedicates. It was irritating, like a clock that ticked too loudly. I'd just started to think about shifting my left arm when she suddenly sucked in a breath, half-sat up, and whispered, "Tvell."

"What?"

"Tvell—I promised them I'd check in. It's been hours." She swallowed. "I'm sorry, I don't—I know everyone's wanting to sleep—will it bother you if I use the command plate? It should be quiet."

I'd never seen a command plate close up; they didn't start training Dedicates with them until they were at least ten years old, and by then I'd already been gone. The part where I was going to have to figure out how to use it after stealing it was something else I'd been carefully not thinking about. Another gift dropping in my lap, now—and one I couldn't afford to turn down. "Yeah," I muttered. "Sure. Go ahead."

"Thank you," the novice murmured back, as if I might have had the choice to say no. I heard cloth rustling under my chin, and felt her shifting as she drew the command plate out. I wished I could see what she was doing. There had been too many Dedicates crowding around earlier for me to get a good look at her hands, and now it was too dark, and my angle was too bad; all I could see was the shadowy top of her head, a bump that was her shoulder and another that was her knees. It didn't seem like she was moving her arms much. Was holding it really all that she had to do?

She had gone still now, a different kind of stillness from before. There was a sense of absence about her that seemed all wrong for a living person. For a moment I couldn't help but think that I was holding a corpse, and had to suppress a jerk of disgust. It *was* unnatural, what she was doing—however the command plate worked, it was grotesque, an abomination—but a normal Dedicate probably saw the sisters send mental orders to their puppets on the daily.

After what felt to me like a long time, I felt a wobble and then a knock against my chest. She'd lifted her chin and banged her forehead against the curve of my breastplate. It must have hurt her at least a little, but she didn't seem bothered. "I was able to reach them," she whispered. "Firzen found Dirk. They're both—they're both alive. They're both all right. We should be able to connect up with them soon."

She was telling me because everyone else was asleep, and because I was there—and because Firzen and Dirk were supposedly my comrades, and she thought I would be happy to know that they were all right. In a way, it was a kind thing for her to do.

And it *was* good news, even for me. The more Dedicates rejoined us, the more Dedicates I could bring back to Levasta. The more Dedicates I brought back, the better chance Levasta had of winning the war.

If Levasta won the war, no Dedicates would be made ever again.

"That's great," I whispered back, and almost meant it.

*　*　*

BARGHEST WOKE TO light filtering in through the mouth of the cave. Sometime in the night, after they'd traded watches with Dreizen, the blizzard had stopped.

They pushed themself to a seat and looked around. They weren't the only one awake. Dreizen seemed to have fallen back asleep after their turn on guard, but Cascabela was standing out past the entrance, Firzen was kneeling by Svanik, and Asher and Titan were frowning over ration packs.

Asher looked better than she had yesterday, so far as Barghest could tell—more color in her face, which Barghest generally understood to be a positive sign for people with faces. And her clothes seemed dry. These were things to pay attention to.

They'd kept watch on Asher as well as they could, but at some point over the long hours of yesterday's march they'd forgotten that the risk of her driving herself to exhaustion wasn't the only thing they needed to worry about. Soft-shelled humans needed clothing, shelter. Exposed skin could be damaged by prolonged exposure to cold or heat, and they lost the ability to generate their own warmth far more rapidly than Dedicates did. These facts all went into strategic planning; they were why human troops needed campfires and extended supply trains and camp followers to do their laundry. Barghest had been an active soldier for nine years, had commanded troops for the last two. None of this was new.

Barghest didn't know which of the Dedicates had been the one to offer Asher a place next to them. When they'd come back in after their watch, it had been far too dark to see anything but a larger bulk with a smaller one curled up next to them. They had not wanted to look long, in any case. It felt wrong in an instinctual way, uncomfortable, like seeing an official wear their formal ruff backwards, or hearing someone swear in chapel.

Improper or not, however, the offer had likely saved Asher's life, and Barghest had not thought to do it. Consciously, Barghest set both their discomfort and the sting of their failure aside to focus on what they should learn from this. Military regulations did not always take extraordinary situations into account. They could do better about remembering that.

At this point, Firzen turned their head and saw Barghest sitting up. "Sir," they said, "if you're awake, can I take another look at your back?"

Asher looked up from her ration packs. "What's wrong with the Sergeant's back?"

Barghest felt a flicker of irritation, and released it with a sigh. There was no point in keeping it hidden; Asher would likely already have seen for herself, if not for chance and the storm. "We all took some damage from the fall yesterday," they answered, and turned around, presenting their back to Firzen. They heard Asher's indrawn breath, and went on, calmly. "I don't think it's particularly serious, but of course I can't see for myself, so I'll let the expert be the judge."

"Um—" Barghest glanced over their shoulder to see her pushing herself to her feet. "I don't want to intrude, but do you mind if I watch the examination? I'd—remember, I'd hoped to learn more about medical conditions that might impact—but it's all right if you're not comfortable with it," she added, quickly.

Intellectual curiosity was better than needless anxiety. "I don't mind," said Barghest.

"Thank you," said Asher, and then turned to Firzen, who was pulling their tools out of the storage compartment in their mechanical arm. "And thank you, as well. For, um, letting me look over your shoulder?"

"Don't mention it, sir," said Firzen, head firmly lowered over their tinderbox. They sounded profoundly uncomfortable, which was more or less the reaction Barghest had expected.

Asher's face changed color a little, but she nodded, and Barghest faced back towards the cave wall. Uncomfortable pressure bloomed on their back as Firzen's upper hands began exploring their way up the damaged section of their carapace, mapping out each dent, assessing how much the warped metal had torn into the muscle underneath. The sensation moved to their shoulders, and then to their neck. Firzen tried to be careful, but they were young, and clumsy still. It was not pleasant. Barghest sat still, and breathed.

After a moment, Asher asked, "What are the risks?"

"Well, um—" Barghest heard pages turning. Firzen must have managed to bring their medical text down with them after the avalanche, and was using their lower hands to read it. "The back itself isn't really very vulnerable, the plating is solid and our muscles heal up quickly, but there's a difficult spot right at the base of the skull—you see? There has to be a separation there between the plates of the back and the helmet, or we couldn't turn our necks, but that's also near where the godstone is embedded, so—"

"It seems dangerous to have it there rather than lower down the back," said Asher. "But—I suppose it has to be there, since the head is where the soul is? Closest to the heavens." Her voice sounded the same as it did during Sor Elena's evening debriefings—like she was consulting an invisible textbook of her own inside her head. "The center of the body has all the base survival impulses, and the soul has, um, thought, and logic, and compassion, and all the decisions that run counter to the body's self-interest. And the spine is the conduit that lets the body submit to the soul. So when someone uses a sympathetic chip to resonate with the godstone at the base of the spine, the body will submit to another soul's decisions, too. Ah, right?"

She was testing herself, Barghest realized. Showing off, maybe, even though Sor Elena was no longer here to impress.

They were grateful for the distraction, anyway. It helped, when injured, to focus on basic theology: the body is like the center of the earth, seething with hunger and fear and lust, ambushing the accomplishments of the soul with tremors and eruptions. You needed the body, as you needed the earth, but if you let it control you then you would never be more than dirt and fire.

Discomfort was a disruption of the body. Overcoming it, with self-control, was a holy act—as holy as submitting to the control of a Sor-Commander.

"Yes, sir," said Firzen, obligingly. "That's what I was taught. And you'd have to get hit at a very specific angle to damage it, but it's important to check anyway." Firzen pulled their hands away; Barghest let out their breath in silent relief. "But it seems the Sergeant is right. I could be wrong, but I don't think there's much to worry about here."

"Really? That's good to hear." The relief in Asher's voice was audible. Perhaps the textbook responses had been a distraction for her as well. "It still looks so... Does it hurt?"

"No," said Barghest. It was not a lie. Dedicates did not

61

feel pain the way unaltered humans did. Discomfort was only discomfort. "Are you finished, Firzen?"

"Yes, Sergeant."

Barghest turned back around, and Asher sat back on her heels, giving them space. "Thank you for allowing me to sit in on your examination," she said. "I appreciated it. I'm going to check in with Tvell now. I think—probably someone should explore the cave system? And then we can decide what to do next."

ASHER TOOK HER hand off the command plate. "The good news," she said, "is that Tvell says they and Dirk are doing fine."

"Tvell *and* Dirk?" said Barghest. "They found each other?"

"Oh—yes, they did—Tvell found Dirk yesterday. I checked in last night." Asher tried for a smile. "They're together now, and making progress."

Part of her had expected to somehow receive answering smiles back, even though she knew it was impossible. Still, Barghest gave a slow nod, and she heard one or two sighs of relief from around the circle. They'd been worried, and now they were less worried. She didn't need their faces to tell her that.

Guilt followed after the glow of satisfaction, as reliable as moths after wool. She could have told everyone about Tvell and Dirk as soon as she woke up, instead of making Barghest and Firzen uncomfortable by intruding on their medical treatment. But there was no use regretting that now. She took a breath, and said, "There's bad news too. From where they are they can see the crevice that we've been using for our path, and unfortunately, it dead-ends.

That means we have two choices: either we backtrack until we can find a route higher up the mountain, or we try to push forward through the underground system here. Titan, what did you find when you went into the caves?"

"I didn't go very far," Titan answered, "but it opens out, for sure. I followed a few of the branches a little ways. There was airflow down most of them, and I heard rushing water down one. And there's enough moss around that I think we could keep torches lit, if we wanted."

"Well done," Asher said, and tried not to feel ridiculous for granting her approval like they had any reason to feel it was worth something. "Um—so, on the maps I studied before we came, there was a network of tunnels that went all the way through the mountain. The army was able to use them six years ago, when we took Green Adam back from Levasta—the Levastani didn't know about the tunnels then, so—that's promising. But after the earthquake, the maps may not be accurate anymore? And even if the tunnels *do* still go all the way through, it's not direct. It would still probably be faster than backtracking, though. And we can replenish our supplies, better than we would outside, since glacial cetraria lichen is edible—"

"Glacial what?" said Titan.

"The moss you found," said Asher. "So well done on that, too." Perhaps this was too much praise for a single Dedicate. She went on, quickly, "The downside is that if it doesn't work out, we'll have to double back twice as far—and being in cave system could be risky if we had another earthquake."

Firzen raised their hand. "Permission to speak, sir?" Asher nodded at them, and they said, "I'd prefer not to go back out into the snow if we can help it. Svanik's injuries—"

"I'm *fine*," snapped Svanik. "I'm ready to go as soon as Dreizen stops snoring over there."

"What? I don't snore." Dreizen sat up from where they'd been sprawled on the ground, and promptly cracked their armored head on the ceiling of the cave. "Ow!"

Svanik snickered.

"Well, that settles it," said Dreizen. "*Svanik* is fine. *I* have a concussion now. But we can all move past it."

"Svanik is not fine," said Firzen, wearily, just as Svanik said, "I told you—"

"Thank you all for your input," said Barghest, which shut everyone else up immediately. "Does anybody else have relevant intelligence to share before the commander makes her decision?"

The Dedicates all shook their heads, which meant that Asher couldn't stall any longer. She looked over at Barghest, hoping for some kind of sign about what they thought she should choose.

Barghest looked back. Their shoulders shifted, lowering. She was fairly sure they *were* in fact sending her a sign, one that any other Dedicate would have known how to read, but she did not understand it.

It didn't matter. She was commander; the decision had to be hers anyway. She squared her own shoulders and looked back at the others. "Since everyone's awake now, we'll leave within the half-hour, just as soon as everyone's had a chance to eat something. And—" She looked back at Svanik, and the broken metal spiking viciously through the protective waxed linen that Firzen had wrapped around their upper arm where the javelin had pierced them. "We'll try the caves."

* * *

64

CASCABELA HAD USED lichen, oil, and a swathe of Asher's shift to transform their lower right hand into a makeshift torch. They held it aloft at the front of the troupe, gathering more lichen with their right hands as they went and feeding it into the flames. Asher and Titan followed behind, then Dreizen, Firzen, and Svanik. Barghest had once again decided to take the rear, in part because they knew the light would be worst there. Better for those more injured to have as much visibility as they could.

Taking the caves was a reasonable decision, given the party's limitations. Barghest was glad that Asher had chosen it, even though the hunching required by the low ceilings sent strange ripples through their battered back.

But Titan was right—soon enough, the caves opened up. The striated rock of the walls took on shifting jewel-tones in the flicker of Cascabela's torch, grays turning to rust, whites shifting to gold. In places, the ceiling cracked open to the sky, and luminous particles of snow drifted gently down in the beams of light that broke through. Patches of black ice shimmered in one angle of view, and disappeared in the next.

"It's like a Holy House," murmured Firzen.

Barghest agreed. It felt like proof that the light of the gods could reach anywhere. They wished that the tramping of metal feet would cease for just a minute, so that they could stand for a while in silence and look up at the cracks of heaven, illuminating the bowels of the earth.

What they said was: "Watch out for the black ice. It may be treacherous."

"Yes, sir," chorused four voices, and then Svanik— almost as if precisely to be contrary—placed their foot wrong and plummeted forward.

The sound that they let out as their damaged arm crashed into the wall was horrible. They staggered and bent over, another hand coming up over the grille of their face as if to stop the noise from escaping.

Firzen was there just an instant too late. "Svanik!"

"It's nothing," Svanik snarled, and pushed themself back to their feet, good arms clutching the injured one as if to cut sensation off at the pass.

"It's not *nothing*!" hissed Firzen. "Stop saying that! I wish it wasn't true—I wish you *did* know better than me about this. I wish you could just stubborn your way through it, but you can't!"

"Through what?" said Barghest, sharply.

Firzen turned to Barghest, the angle of their head tense and miserable. "Sir—their injury's gotten infected. I think they may be septic."

"Are you sure?"

An infected wound was one of the worst things that could happen to a Dedicate. The metal that encased them—that was supposed to protect them from injury in the first place—also made it fiendishly difficult to reach damaged tissue and safely remove it. Once infection set in, treating the wound required a long and complicated surgery that the patient didn't always survive. Dedicates were stronger and more resilient than almost any ordinary human, but there were limits.

Firzen nodded, unhappiness written in every sagging line of their body. "I'm sure. I thought so yesterday, but I was hoping I was wrong. But now—"

They turned to look at Asher. "Sir, I really don't want to risk operating with a field kit. When we reach the army, they'll have real medics—experienced ones, I mean—and good equipment. But if we go too fast, and push them too hard, I don't know—I don't know what's right to do."

Barghest saw Asher swallow; saw her shoulders brace to take the weight of this responsibility, as well. But her voice, when she spoke, was steady. "Sergeant Barghest."

"Yes, sir?"

"You've been in the field longer than many, is that right? Do you have any experience to offer?"

"I've seen such injuries before, yes," said Barghest, after a bare moment's pause. They were grateful that control over their own voice had always come easily to them. "I've seen Dedicates recover from them, with proper treatment."

What happened without proper treatment didn't have to be said. Asher nodded, and turned to Firzen. "We'll go as fast as we can, then."

Firzen looked down. Barghest was fairly sure they wouldn't have been content with either answer. There simply wasn't a good one.

Perhaps Asher was learning to read their unhappiness too, because she said, "I promised to get you all through here, and I meant it."

"Not all of us," said Cascabela.

They stood a little ahead, and they didn't look back as they spoke, but it was clear they meant to be heard. Their carapace was a black bulk wreathed in smoke from the flame that burned in their palm. They looked unhelpfully like an allegory.

Despite all their best intentions, Barghest hadn't managed to find time to talk to them last night, which meant this was Barghest's fault. "Cascabela," they began.

"You're right." Asher cut Barghest off, taking a step

towards Cascabela. "Not all of us. Aconite and Alft and Zekzen and Baselard—" She said the names without pausing or stumbling. The torchlight caught the hollows of her eyes and the yellowing bruise on her cheek. She looked like an allegory, too. "I haven't forgotten them."

"You didn't *know* them."

"Soldiers die, Cascabela," said Titan. Their voice was light and edged. "If you're assigning blame, how about the Sor-Commander? Or whoever gave *her* orders?"

That was the point—already past the point—at which Barghest needed to shut the conversation down. They had the words ready, but they were caught in their throat, pinned by the spear that had gone through Aconite.

In the silence where Barghest's voice should have been, Titan went on: "And it's not like the novice is habited. Right now, she's just as likely to die as any of us."

"Apparently," rasped Svanik, "not *just* as likely as me."

There was a pause before they added, "That was a joke."

"Svanik," said Dreizen, "I don't want to discourage your attempts at humor, but—"

"We don't *want* you to die," said Firzen, louder than Barghest had ever heard them speak, "and it's not *funny!*"

"Who wants to live forever?" muttered Svanik, and leaned back against the wall.

"You'd better *try*," Firzen retorted. "Your life belongs to the gods, or did you forget that? If you don't care enough about yourself, you've got a *duty* to—"

"Fight another day?" Cascabela swung suddenly around, the fire swinging with them. Patches of ice on the wall blazed and vanished as the light shifted over them. Unbidden, the first words of the First Text passed through Barghest's mind, as they had first read them by flickering lamplight as a child in the Holiest House: *when it all began there was nothing but earth and fire.* "And die in the next battle? Or watch someone else—"

"The gods play rough with their toys," said Titan, looking at Cascabela.

"The gods," said Firzen, tightly, "aren't children. They don't play games. They gave us a *purpose*—"

"Oh, sure," said Titan. "Glorious."

Dreizen's laugh rang a discordant note in the charged atmosphere of the caves. "Only the holiest of cannon fodder, that's us."

Metal ground against metal, and Barghest realized their hands had formed into fists.

"That," they said, louder than they meant, "is *enough*."

These conversations happened in every unit, from time to time. Of course they did. Even for the most faithful, faith had its limits. But they didn't happen in front of senior officers, and they *never* happened in front of the sisters.

All of their troops should know better than this.

But Dreizen and Titan were still wet behind the ears, and Cascabela was grieving. And Asher was young enough, vulnerable enough, that she didn't seem quite like a commander. The barriers were breaking down, and all of them, Asher included, were afraid.

Barghest understood. They understood all too well. But this journey would finish, and their troops would join the army, and they would have to know what it meant to be a soldier, with a soldier's discipline. Levasta was still coming. The war did depend on them. Whatever the justice or injustice of the sacrifices that the gods had asked of them, that much didn't change.

Barghest had never liked feeling angry. It seemed a

waste of time. This flash of fury at the other Dedicates for forcing Barghest to be the person who pushed them back down into silence—this, also, would pass.

WE WERE MOSTLY quiet for the next few hours, as we picked our way through the caves, and quiet as we found a place to make camp. I couldn't stop turning over the argument from earlier, wondering if I'd made a slip. Probably I shouldn't have chimed in at all. But it was getting harder to remember how this Dedicated version of me was supposed to think or act—especially when the others kept saying things I never thought to hear from someone under the sisters' control. The only one of us who was still behaving like a perfect soldier was Barghest. I wasn't sure Barghest could act anything *but* perfect.

Even as I thought that, I heard Barghest's voice behind me, and turned at the sound of a name that wasn't mine.

I was expecting a lecture. Instead, Barghest said, "I promised you a practice match, didn't I? I apologize that we've had to delay it until now."

They didn't sound as if they were angry at me for what I'd said. The brief wave of relief I felt about that made me furious.

I tried to pitch my voice light, as I turned. "Is there room?" But of course there was. The novice had somehow navigated us to a cavern that was bigger than the training yards I'd practiced in back in Levasta. She really was turning out to be useful. Keeping her alive last night had been a solid tactical decision.

Somehow that made me even angrier than before.

But I couldn't afford to be too angry, or it would start to show. A little controlled violence might take the edge off. "All right, Sergeant," I said, and pushed myself to my feet. "Thanks for the offer. I lost my axe in the avalanche, though, so I'll need to borrow—"

"Use one of mine," said Barghest, and handed me theirs—the right-sided one, more or less identical to the one I'd lost. My dominant pair of hands, and, I was pretty sure, theirs as well.

They led me to a corner of the cave, away from the others. The novice glanced up as we went past her and then looked politely away. No one else came to watch us either, even though it wasn't like there was much other entertainment on offer. Maybe Barghest had told them not to look, or maybe they just thought it would be rude.

In Levasta, dozens of people usually came to watch whenever I sparred with anybody. I was the only Dedicate they could learn anything about. I didn't much mind, there. Levasta had given my mother and me a lot. They deserved some kind of return on their investment. Being watched wasn't the worst thing—especially when I knew I was going to do well.

Here, I would have hated it. I was clearly about to get trounced. The only question was how polite Barghest was going to be about it. Not very, I hoped. Even if they were better than me, at least I could land one or two hard blows.

I braced the axe in my two right hands, and took a starting stance.

For a few moments, we just circled each other, getting each other's measure. We were almost the same height, but I had a finger or two on Barghest, who was on the shorter side of the narrow spectrum within which Dedicates fall. It still deeply strange to face someone across a sparring floor and look them almost exactly in the eyes. My usual opponents hardly ever came up above my shoulder. At least I wouldn't have to worry too much about low attacks.

And of course as soon as I thought that Barghest came in low on my right, their axe a gray slash in the air as it swung towards my knee. It took me completely by surprise—I hadn't seen them bend their shoulders at all—and I jumped backwards, bringing my own axe down to block. As soon as our weapons clanged on each other, I knew that had been a mistake. Using my blade to push my opponent back had always served me well before, but I couldn't pit my strength against Barghest and expect to get anywhere. By the time I'd gotten my weapon free again, they'd already turned to put themself in my blind spot. I spun, knowing that I was almost certainly not going to be in time to stop whatever move they'd put in motion—

But they only slowed and came in again, the same way. This time, I stepped aside instead of trying to block. As we fell back into circling, I had more of a chance to see what they'd been doing: instead of swinging the axe high with the upper arm dominant, as I usually did, they were leveraging the mechanical power of their lower left arm, using the upper arm as a guide only. Because a Dedicate's lower arm joined under the ribcage rather than at the shoulder, they hadn't had to lower their posture the way a normal person would to get under my guard. That was why I hadn't seen it coming.

I made a couple of feints towards them as we went round each other; the first two they dodged, and the third they met with their own axe high. To show them I'd been paying attention, I tried switching the balance to my lower arm so the axe could tilt and slide underneath theirs. I was clumsy—generally I only used the lower arms to add power and stability to a standard thrust—and they didn't have any trouble avoiding my attack.

Then they met my blade again with theirs, giving me a chance at another try.

It was better this time. I could feel it, and they saw it, too; next time they didn't come at me the same way, but switched the axe back down, going back to the lower style. Once again, it caught me by surprise—it would take me a while to learn those tells—but I was faster in responding, and the swing I took at the shoulder they'd left open made me almost, a little, proud of myself. Barghest must have thought it was all right too, because instead of repeating the same stroke, they moved around, and tried the attack from the other side: could I block it, then? Could I find the space they left open?

When Barghest offered a training match, I expected to be told all the ways I was failing. Instead, they were asking questions with their movements, and guiding me to the answers. With each one, I felt like I could glimpse a world of potential in my body that I hadn't understood before. I'd had good teachers in Levasta, but they'd trained me the same way they'd train anyone who looked just like themselves. There hadn't been anyone to show me the full extent of what I could be—

—which was a better blade, of course; nothing but a better blade. That was all any of us would ever be, to the Levastani or the Cesteli. In Cesteli hands, I could have become a finer weapon than I ever would in Levasta, but at least the Levastani would give me some say in how I was used.

Barghest and their axe were now on my right. I saw the stretch of their upper arm out of the corner of my eye and lifted my axe to block, planning to use the tilt they'd shown me to slip away from under them. But instead of the high attack I'd expected, they came in low towards my knees again, the same attack they'd made at the very beginning of the bout. Having seen that move twice already, I should have been able to counter it—I think they expected me to counter it—but I'd gotten distracted, and didn't move fast enough. At the last minute, they turned their axe so the back of it hit my knees, and I went down flat on my face.

I just lay there for a moment, breathing hard and thinking about the mistake I'd made. Then I heaved a sigh and rolled over onto my back. Barghest reached out an arm to pull me to my feet and gave me a nod of respect, just as if I'd been any kind of real opponent for them. "Thank you for the practice."

"You were doing me a favor, Sergeant," I said, "and we both know it. Thank you." My earlier anger had all drained out of me; now I just felt sad. Barghest, it turned out, was a good teacher. It was wrong that all of their patient care should be directed towards me, who was deceiving them; it was worse to see their gifts shackled to the cage of a carapace and a command plate.

What might this person have been, if their chance to be a person had not been stolen by the Cesteli gods?

But there was nothing I could do about that. Their fate, like mine, had been sealed years ago. I offered them their right-handed axe back, but Barghest shook their head. "You should keep it, in case there's trouble," they said. "If we have the space—if you're willing—we'll do it again tomorrow."

*　　*　　*

How's Dirk healing?

They're doing all right, answered Tvell, in the bottom of their throat. *Still limping, but they're getting their stamina back. You know it's hard to keep us down for long!*

If Asher opened her own eyes, she would see Svanik laid out like a fallen war hero surrounded by flowers—Firzen had packed a bed of soft lichen around them to keep them from banging their arm in the night. She swallowed down her guilt and answered, *That's right. I'm glad to hear it.*

This was the fourth time she'd visited Tvell through the command plate. Every time, it became a little less frightening; she was learning to alight in their body as a visiting presence, a blink of the eye and a whisper in the throat. Subvocalization was starting to feel natural. She was almost certain that she did not currently stand any risk of overbalancing them off the mountain. *We're settling in now for the night,* she told them, *long enough that everyone can split watches and still get some sleep. You both should do the same? I'll let you know when we're moving again.*

Thank you, sir, said Tvell, and Asher lifted her fingers from the command plate. She breathed in deeply, resettling her self into her own body, and became at once unpleasantly aware that said body, unlike Tvell's, was extremely cold.

She'd selected a cave for the night based on the notes from the map she'd memorized, which indicated the space had been stable for the past several hundred years. Its size was incidental, but also in some ways advantageous. Barghest had been pleased to have the space to conduct training—the first time in fact that Asher had ever felt confident about recognizing that Barghest was pleased, a satisfaction in its own right. However, it also meant that the Dedicates' machinery didn't put out nearly enough heat to warm the entire area. Dreizen had gotten a fire going to stew lichen into gruel for dinner, but the fuel that the Dedicates had gathered over the course of the day burned bright, not hot, and wouldn't last the night.

Asher's eyes fell wistfully on her Dedicates, arranged in their various configurations against the walls of the cave: Barghest standing watch by the entrance; Firzen and Dreizen sprawled against each other near Svanik like a pair of very stiff puppies; Cascabela alone on the far side of the cave, curled up in a ball, incongruously childlike; Titan, closest to her, with their back propped against the wall and their expressionless faceplate tilted up towards the ceiling.

She looked away quickly, rubbing her hands briskly together to warm them. She couldn't ask to impose. It felt like she hadn't been warm in years, but in reality it had only been fourteen hours or so. She wasn't wet anymore, and between her cloak, her robes and her shift she had plenty of layers to prevent herself from losing too much body heat while she slept.

"Can't sleep?" said Titan, without moving from where they sat.

Asher jerked her head up. She wished the heat of embarrassment in her cheeks actually translated into any useful body warmth. "Um—"

"You can shiver like a martyr over there if you want," said Titan, "but you know it's not strictly necessary, right?"

Asher hesitated.

Last night, she'd been too tired and cold to feel much

awkwardness about falling asleep curled up next to a Dedicate. Now she was still tired, and still cold, but awake enough to make decisions that were based on something besides the requirements of survival.

"It's—really kind of you, Titan, but if you'd prefer—um, your own space—"

Looking at her face as she grappled for words, Titan laughed. "I'm not saying I'd be volunteering if there was a better option. If you'd rather one of the others—"

Asher shook her head, firmly. She wasn't going to march up to any Dedicate who hadn't offered and demand to use them as a pillow.

"Smart," said Titan. They stretched their arms up and then shifted position, stretching out against the cave wall. "Dreizen has the worst snore in the battalion."

Asher snickered, and then immediately felt guilty. She wasn't supposed to be playing favorites. She carefully arranged her cloak around her and inched into the circle of heat that Titan generated, until she could feel their chestplate against her back. Their two right arms draped carefully over her, warm weights pressing down on her shoulder. The now familiar rust-and-blood Dedicate smell overwhelmed the musty odor of the caves.

It didn't feel comfortable—it couldn't possibly—but it felt safe.

That made her uncomfortable, too.

The gods couldn't protect their people directly. Ascending, they left the physical world behind; they could not remain gods and return. The Dedicates defended Cesteli State in their stead, acting as the gods could not, protecting those who could not protect themselves. People like Asher and the other novices, and the habited sisters with their delicate godstone machinery, and all the families that they'd left behind. All the people who'd Dedicated their children so that Cesteli State could survive.

It was a holy compact. None of the sisters in the Holiest Houses would have used the words that Dreizen or Cascabela had, or spoken of their purpose with Titan's ironic twist. But it was true that the country sheltered behind the Dedicates, as Asher was sheltering next to Titan now, and a truth didn't become a lie just because you used a different name for it.

Earlier, she had felt ashamed for keeping silent, but she knew that if she had put herself back into that conversation it would have immediately become a different one—and, coward-like, not one that she was sure she wanted to have, at least not with the whole group.

Starting just with Titan, who had been kind to her today, might be easier.

"Titan," she murmured—half-hoping, despite herself, that they'd already fallen asleep, and wouldn't answer. Glad she wasn't looking into their face, though she wouldn't have been able to read it anyway.

"Yes?"

"Would you rather be like the habited sisters? Just soul, no body, and, um, immortal, probably?"

She felt the frame around her shift—a tension in the upper right arm. "Why talk about things that won't happen?"

"Well—it's not impossible. Anyone can become— there's a reason they don't make Dedicates that way, you know. Not just because the habits break more easily, but because you're all so young when you're Dedicated, and taking the soul's habit is, um, a thing you really have to want, spiritually? Not eating or sleeping or anything, forever, and a kid wouldn't understand that—but if an adult Dedicate wanted to take the habit, and become a sister, I don't see why they—she couldn't? Anyway—I don't know if it's ever happened. But I can't think of anything that would prevent it."

Titan let out a long exhale, far enough above Asher's head that she heard rather than felt it. "I don't know that I'd put money on that."

Asher started to shrug and then banged her shoulder against Titan's arms. "You didn't answer my question?"

It was another moment before Titan answered. "I like sleeping. And eating. Even the mush we get—well, sometimes you get flavors of mush that are all right, actually. Better than nothing."

"That makes sense." She swallowed. An answer seemed to deserve an answer. "I do, too."

"Do what?"

"Like sleeping. And eating."

"You're saying you don't want to be habited?"

"I don't—"

She broke off. She'd always come top in her classes. Her teachers were looking to groom her for command. That was why she was here in the bowels of this mountain, on her way to the front—so she could get the experience she needed; so she could learn repair work, and tactics in the field. So she could prepare to take the habit and join the war.

They would never force her. The soul's habit was a voluntary renunciation of the sins and desires of the flesh, a sign that one had taken one step closer to the gods. It *had* to be chosen; if it wasn't, there would be nothing sacred about it. To force it upon anyone would be blasphemous.

"I don't know," she said, finally.

"You don't *know*?"

There didn't seem any way to explain. She tried anyway. "Taking the habit—it means, you know, that you've mastered yourself. And everyone sees that, and everyone knows you've earned the respect you get for it. It's—it's the greatest thing a person can achieve? If you think about it spiritually, anyway. I mean, if you count spiritual achievements as the most important."

There were sisters of the flesh, many of them. There had been sisters of the flesh since long before Sor Ana of Aurelie had fired ceramic in her own shape and become the first to take the soul's habit a century ago. Like their habited sisters, they lived, worked and prayed in the Holiest Houses, and, unlike the habited, died there. In peacetime, all had served together as scholars, scientists, and artists, working towards the greater edification of the soul in all its forms; as caretakers and teachers, also, of the poor and orphaned who were thrown on the mercy of the Holiest House.

Now, in wartime, the unhabited carried on their work within the cloisters as best they could. They did not act as a voice for virtue on the battlefield or in treaty halls. They did not command fear from the enemy, or awe from Cesteli's own councilmembers and petty bourgeois. They were good women, virtuous women, but they didn't achieve the soul's full potential. They didn't approach the gods.

But they ate, and they slept.

"Well," said Titan. "I guess it's nice to have the choice."

It was a conversation-ending sort of remark. Asher could close her eyes, and go to sleep. But the idea of leaving it there, like she didn't care about the faint condescension in Titan's voice, made a worm twist in her stomach. She didn't want them to think she was the kind of person who didn't care.

"How, um… How did you come to be Dedicated?"

For a moment, she thought Titan wouldn't answer. When they did, their voice was odd, nearly as blank as Barghest's. "Me? I'm a war orphan."

"Oh," said Asher—almost wishing she hadn't asked, wondering what she could possibly say next. "Your parents were…?"

"My ma was in the army—that was in the early days of the war, before they had Dedicates out on the front."

The part of Asher that always had to be head of the class wanted to point out that this was obvious, since the first Dedicates had only come of age to be deployed ten years ago. She had a lot of practice at stifling that part of herself.

"She fell pregnant with a year left on her service," Titan went on, "so she came back to have me, left me with a pair of aunts, and went back to the front. Or so I'm told." Their voice was shifting back towards their usual amiable tones, as if it was a story that had happened to somebody else entirely. "But the plague got the aunts, and when the hospital wrote Ma, all they got back was a form letter—missing-presumed. So the nurses Dedicated me, and here I am."

"I—um, do you remember her? Or your aunts?"

"Sir," said Titan, kindly, "I was a year old, tops."

"Oh," said Asher.

"Now maybe you holy sisters can meditate or something to access holy baby thoughts, but—"

"Yes, all *right*," said Asher, "I get it," and Titan gave a small snort of laughter.

"Well," they said, "what about you?"

"What about me?"

"I just, Asher—excuse the disrespect—"

"No, please," said Asher, hastily.

"—it isn't a particularly Cesteli name, is it?"

"Um, no," said Asher. "No, it's—" She hesitated over which term to use, and went with the one most common in the Cesteli language; Titan probably wouldn't have heard 'Gedank.' "—it's a Vapenzi name. I'm named for my grandfather, he was—he settled here when the Vapenzi were expelled from Karyous."

"I kind of wondered," said Titan. "And your Vapenzi grandpa, he didn't mind you joining the Holiest House?"

"Well," said Asher. "He's very, um. I mean, my grandmother's Cesteli. And he wanted his family to do well and be safe, and that's easier if—anyway, it's not like—you know, the faiths aren't that different. It's important to both of them that, um, you're generally virtuous, and behave well, and unselfishly?"

"The *gods* are different," said Titan. "That's pretty important, I'd think."

"Well, it's really interesting, actually. Some of the founding parables are—you know the one about the woman and the rabbit, the first selfless act? It's the same story, really." She could hear her voice warming at the chance to have an old debate—something as familiar to her as her grandfather's fireplace, that she'd thought through and formed opinions on—with a new person. "Only you know, for us it's a story about the first person to ascend to godhood, about *escaping* the earth, and for the Vapenzi, it's a story about how the gods of the earth were cruel, until a person taught them how they might not be—it's about how we can inspire the gods to be

82

better, by our acts. Which is a nice idea. But when you think about the world since then, it's hard to believe the gods have gotten any kinder? The world is just as difficult as it always was. The Cesteli version just, it makes more sense to me?"

"But your grandfather still wanted you to be named for him," said Titan. "To have a Vapenzi name."

"Well," said Asher, a little uncomfortably, "it's—you know. He's still my *grandfather*. Anyway, when I become a full sister, I'll be Sor something. Maybe Sor Benita, that means—" She broke off. "Wait... how did you recognize my name as Vapenzi?"

Titan was silent for a long moment. Finally, they said, "When I was really little, before—" They moved their hand, in a vague gesture that almost banged her nose— "I had curly hair like yours."

"Oh," Asher said.

It didn't answer her question—they'd already said they were too little then to remember—but another question probably was not the right thing, right now. Once again, she found herself grasping desperately for what *would* be the right thing, the thing to make them like her: maybe my family knew your family, before they all died? You were probably a cute baby, before you were metal?

She drew in a breath. "If you want to talk more, about... I used to talk a lot about religion, with my grandfather. I mean, not tonight. It's late and we should sleep. But if you want to, later—"

"I'm in a carapace, and you're a Sor-Commander," said Titan. "At this point, I don't know that it really matters."

After just long enough that she was convinced that she'd said the absolute wrong thing after all, they added, "But thanks."

*   *   *

ASHER FELL ASLEEP soon after that conversation, but I stayed up, thinking about my gods and the jokes that they played.

This—me, helping Asher now, so that I could betray her later—was exactly the kind of thing they liked. If any god was watching me lie uncomfortably awake so that my enemy could sleep warmly, perhaps they'd feel ashamed; perhaps they'd think they could stand to put themselves out a little more to make things easy for us poor mortals, whether or not it amused them. But if they kept watching, they'd see that my kindness had been self-serving. They would see they had nothing to learn from me. They'd laugh with relief, and then laugh again the next time some fool accepted what looked like a divine helping hand—a welcome respite, a path that seemed easy—only to find that doing so had thoroughly fucked them over.

Asher's Gedank name and grandfather didn't seem to matter much to her. There wasn't any reason they should matter to me, either, except that it meant the gods were twice as likely to be paying attention. They took a special interest because the Gedank were the only people who had ever tried to teach them anything. Since they knew we were trying to reach them, everything we did meant more to them—like reading a letter written to you, rather than someone else's mail. That was how my mother had explained it to me, anyway.

Not so long after my mother found me again, when all her ideas were new and I still didn't understand most of them, I'd asked her if the Gedank gods had been angry to see me Dedicated. In claiming me, hadn't the Cesteli gods stolen something that was rightfully theirs? My mother

84

told me that the Cesteli gods weren't real, and that our gods couldn't possibly have been as angry as she was; a parent's fury beats a god's any day. I didn't realize until later that she hadn't really answered my question at all.

The truth is that when my gods saw me receive the terrible gift of this body, they'd probably found it hilarious.

In the end I did manage to snatch some sleep before Barghest woke me for watch, but it wasn't anywhere near enough. Between that, and the stiffness from getting slammed into the floor during our sparring match, I started off the next day in a bad mood that only got worse as it went on. It didn't help that I kept catching Asher stealing glances at me, as if she wanted to make sure she wouldn't mistake me for one of the others. When Firzen complained about Dreizen's snoring she shot me a little shared-joke smile.

I didn't want to share a joke with her. I didn't want to like her at all. She talked about my people like they were strangers, and my religion like it was a thought experiment; she had given herself freely to the gods that had stolen me, and right then I wished she would fuck off and die on her own without forcing me to dirty my hands with it. I turned away, and the smile faltered and disappeared.

Fortunately for me—if not anyone else—the passages started narrowing in on us after that, and soon everyone was too busy squeezing through holes and clambering over rock piles to spare any energy for conversation. Every few minutes we had to stop so Cascabela could get the light going again after accidentally extinguishing it against the wall, or Firzen and Dreizen could help Svanik through a pass without jarring their arm. When we finally hit a passageway that we couldn't get through, it felt inevitable to me, but I saw Asher's face crumbling like it was the end of the world.

She had Cascabela come up to the front with the torch, then stood there staring at the heap of fallen stones in front of us as if she could find a way through with the power of her mind alone. Finally, she drew a deep breath and turned around. "All right," she said, wearily. "We'll backtrack and take a different way."

Dreizen looked towards Svanik, then swiveled back. "But—wouldn't it be faster to try and move the rocks? If we worked to clear it—"

"Dreizen," said Barghest, sharply. "The Commander gave an order."

"I do see what you're saying," said Asher, at the same time—then coughed, and gave Barghest an embarrassed look. When Barghest didn't say anything else, she went on, "But I'm worried more of this tunnel could come down. We just can't trust it's stable enough? Sorry. I'd like to give everyone a rest, but I don't think it's safe to stay here."

"Who needs a rest?" demanded Svanik, and started back down the passage we'd just climbed up to get here. Firzen let out a yelp and went chasing after them, which got the rest of us moving quick.

It was much worse going back. Seeing everything over again made it feel like one of those nightmares where you forget that waking up is a possibility. For a while, the only sound was the skittering of displaced pebbles and the clang of rock on metal, punctuated by more hisses of pain from Svanik as we banged into all the same outcroppings as we had on the way up. Eventually Dreizen and Firzen started up with an endless muttered stream of shared jokes and do-you-remembers centered around people with Karyozi-style names like theirs, Alft and Zibm and Zekzen. I suppose they were trying to keep each other's spirits up. It was working at least somewhat, to judge by the occasional bout of nervous giggling, and incidentally made me want to strangle them both.

Ahead of me, Cascabela's shoulders had gone so stiff that all their arms looked mechanical. They didn't seem to be enjoying the double comedy act any more than I was. I wondered which of us would break first, but in the end it was Svanik who snapped. "Would you shut up about them already? Alft was an airhead, and Zekzen was an ashpit. What does it matter?" Their voice cracked, then went on, harsh. "They *died*."

I hadn't heard the word 'ashpit' used like that in at least ten years. A memory hit me with sudden force: the taste of soap bubbles in my mouth, Sor Maravilla's hand on my ear, as she lectured me and one of the others—Talus, maybe?—for slinging profanity at each other inside the Holiest House. We must have been seven or eight, since our mouths had still been accessible. There was a do-you-remember, if I'd had anyone to share it with.

"*You're* an ashpit," said Dreizen, grimly hanging onto their bantering tone, "and we like you, too, gods know why—"

Barghest's voice came in a low warning rumble: "Dreizen," they said, and Dreizen finally—thankfully—shut up.

For a moment, silence fell again.

Because this was just the kind of day we were having, it lasted just long enough to let us all clearly hear the gut-wrenching sound of something screaming off in the distant dark.

* * *

ASHER'S HEART ROSE, as the tunnel around her erupted into noise once more.

"Flaming ashes—"

"What *was* that?"

"Crocutas," Asher whispered.

Dreizen was the only one who heard her over the general cacophony. "Sorry—cro-*whats*?"

"Crocutas." Asher cleared her throat. "Ah—cave hyenas? It's good news."

"Oh," said Dreizen. "Right. Yes. Thank you, sir. If you wouldn't mind explaining, how exactly is that good news?"

The others were all listening now too. Asher fought to look as if she had been expecting something like this all along. "Well—crocutas can't live entirely underground. They're trogloxenes—they go outside to hunt. And they're large enough that any exits that work for them will probably work for us, too. So if we're able to track where they are, it should lead us back to—it means there's—it will make it easier to find a route out."

They took three wrong turns before they found the first sign of the crocutas—a mess of droppings, long-dried, and a few chewed splinters of bone—but after that, the passages got larger, and the going easier, as she had hoped. Asher took a few deep, relieved breaths, and then rapidly switched back to shallow ones. The smell that the crocutas left was thick in her nostrils.

Then: "HYENAS!" shouted Cascabela, from the front of the line, and the light went out.

Asher started blindly forward, and immediately banged her nose against the dented metal of Barghest's back-plate. "Stay behind me, sir," Barghest cautioned, and then started calling out further instructions: "Troops, draw in! Circle around the Commander. Don't let them draw you out alone. Cascabela, *retreat!*"

The cavern was pitch-black and full of noise: hyena-wails, snarls and whines, and the crashing of Dedicate feet on the cave floor. Barghest in front of her was a patch of deeper darkness, faintly distinguishable. She put a hand on their back to make sure she didn't lose track of them, sharp bent iron scraping her palm, and tried to think over the hammering of her heart in her ears. Hyenas should be nothing to a Dedicate. Nothing got past all that armor that wasn't very pointy and traveling very fast. Her troops should make quick work of them. If only it wasn't so dark, and they didn't have so many wounded—

Hyenas liked to target the wounded. And they had one of the strongest bites of any wild creature; they could crush bone. Could they crush metal? She didn't know. They were clever, they coordinated their attacks, but surely they couldn't be as coordinated as a group of trained soldiers, with human intelligence. That was the whole point of Dedicates, that they were intelligent, and independent, but also coordinated. That someone could coordinate them.

And here she was, the person who was meant to do the coordinating, huddling behind her sergeant and doing nothing of use whatsoever.

She took her fingers off Barghest so that she could fumble the command plate out of her pocket, and turned it around in her hands, trying to ascertain by touch and memory whose chip was located where. The empty slots were on the bottom. She could feel the hollow divots with her fingers. If she moved her hand to the right from there, she'd hit Tvell. The left, she thought, ought to be Barghest—but she shrank from inserting herself into Barghest's head; they were in command right now far more than she was.

She put her thumb down on the next chip past Barghest's.

Stillness resolved disorientingly into motion—her arms were swinging, her knees lunging, momentum carrying the actions forward. The power in her arms was incredible, but one leg felt draggy and heavier than the other; *Dreizen,* she thought, as her axe came crashing down on the skull of the hyena.

Sir?

Don't mind me. Dedicates had better dark vision than she did; even with the grille over Dreizen's eyes, she could start putting together a dim picture of the battle. Dreizen was next to Barghest. Just ahead, Firzen and Titan fought together, with Svanik protected between them. As for Cascabela—Cascabela was far up in the narrows of the tunnel leading outwards. She couldn't see how many hyenas they were fending off alone, but she thought it was at least three. They showed no signs of wanting to move backwards to a more sustainable position.

As she watched through Dreizen's eyes, one of the hyenas grabbed one of Cascabela's broken lower arms between their teeth and pulled it hard, like a dog with a stick.

"Cascabela! *Get back here!*"

Barghest's voice came simultaneously from next to her and in front of her. The sensation was so dizzying that she jerked her thumb off the plate, double vision receding until all she could see once more was the jagged dark mass of Barghest's back.

The hyenas sounded terrifyingly close, but that didn't matter. Barghest and Dreizen would protect her. Her duty was to oversee the battle from a broader vantage point, to provide perspective and tactical planning, and to ensure that there were as few losses as possible.

Cascabela might ignore Barghest, but they couldn't ignore her.

Was it Cascabela or Titan's chip next to Dreizen's? She put her thumb down on the next chip on the plate—and saw, felt, heard nothing, except with her own ears and eyes.

Nothing? That couldn't be right. She tried again, pressing her thumb down harder, squeezing her eyes shut, holding her breath—

Still she saw nothing. Still she felt nothing, except an echoing emptiness. The sounds of battle seemed very far away. She was drifting, without a second anchor to cling to. It felt almost peaceful, like meditation, or the moment right before sleep—

She heard something slam against the wall of the cave and jerked back into herself, heart pounding.

Something had gone very wrong. Was that what it would feel like to send her spirit into someone who had died?

But there was no time to investigate, not when the sickening clash of teeth and claws on metal still echoed throughout the cave. Before she had time to think better of it, she moved her thumb to the next chip, and felt the now familiar draw towards another person—real, anchored, with right arms hanging useless, and left arms grimly fending off three hyenas at once.

Cascabela.

Cascabela hacked away steadily, without responding.

Cascabela—the Sergeant thinks you should retreat? To draw the hyenas into the bigger cavern where the others can help you better. Didn't you hear them?

Their mechanical arm didn't hurt, exactly, but the pressure as the hyena pulled on it was deeply unpleasant nonetheless, in ways that were sideways-adjacent to the kind of pain that Asher was used to.

She reached out with Cascabela's lower left arm to pull the hyena away and bash it against the side of the rock. It was easier than she'd expected it to be. Cascabela didn't falter or struggle to compensate, the way Tvell did when she stepped into their body; their legs moved smoothly to accommodate the motion she'd chosen, while their upper arm kept up a single-handed defense.

They were used to this, she realized. They'd had commanders in their head before. The arm she was using moved like her own, and while she knew she wasn't using it as effectively as Cascabela would have, their strength was still enough to force the hyena loose. The pressure in her—Cascabela's—mechanical right arm released. In her own body, she gasped.

Then she realized that there was a hole in Cascabela's defense that had previously been filled by the constant movement of two blades. Any moment now, they could be overwhelmed.

Cascabela! You need to retreat, now! That's an order!

For a long, terrible moment, she was afraid that they would somehow manage not to obey—that she would have to take control of their whole body, and walk them backwards step by heavy step, feeling the weight of their sullen silence in her head all the while.

But: *Yes, sir,* they answered. They took one step back, and then another.

Thank you, said Asher, before she could stop herself, and then fled back to the uncomplicated safety of her own body.

The noise of the battle raged around her. She stood behind a wall of Dedicates, and waited for it to end.

AFTER TWO DAYS underground, the sunlight struck Barghest like a blow. They started to lower the visor inside their grille, then, instead, raised a hand to shield their eyes. It was good to remember how bright the world could be.

When they looked back, they saw Asher behind them reaching her arms up to the sky, shaking out the muscles in her arms. She jumped when she caught their gaze, looking guilty, and brought her arms down again to her sides. Barghest wasn't sure why; there was nothing wrong with stretching, except that a habited sister didn't need to do it.

Asher coughed, and said, "All right—let's stop here for a bit, before we get too far from the caves?" She glanced at Barghest, who gave her a slight nod. In the bright crystal blue at the top of the world, it was hard to believe that the weather was likely to turn sour again, but Barghest knew how fickle fair skies could be. They were glad that Asher was beginning to learn that too.

She went on, "If someone could strip the carcasses while I check in with Tvell—"

"Mmm," said Dreizen, and let the hyena corpse they were carrying drop to the snow. "Carrion gruel for dinner. Everyone's favorite."

"Better us eating them than the other way around." Titan slung their own hyena down next to Dreizen's.

"Think of it as revenge." They pulled a knife from their arm and let it hang carelessly in the air as they looked down. Barghest's opinion of whoever had trained Titan was growing worse by the day. Blade etiquette wasn't something that should be skimped.

"Easier said than done, right?" Dreizen leaned over, heedless of the knife. "Where do you even start with something that strange-looking?"

"I'm going to say—right here?" Titan brought the knife down, with cavalier confidence.

Firzen threw a hand in front to block it. "Look, you don't—" Firzen sighed, and knelt between Titan and Dreizen. "I'll do it. Just—maybe watch, so you know how to do it yourselves next time?"

Asher settled down on a rock with her eyes closed, command plate in her hands. Barghest looked at Firzen, slicing open the hyena with quiet competence, while Dreizen and Titan watched; looked at Svanik, twitchy and too quiet, staring at the hyena corpses like they still might do them an injury; looked at Cascabela, standing a little apart, and went over to them.

"Cascabela, come with me a moment."

There was reluctance written in the set of Cascabela's shoulders, but they followed Barghest around the edge of the rocks, just out of view from the others.

This conversation would have been easier if they'd had it earlier. Barghest could have listened more, and talked less. They were past that point now. Barghest said, "You were slow in the caves."

"Sir—"

"I had to repeat a direct order three times before you obeyed."

Cascabela's gaze dropped to their feet.

"Cascabela," said Barghest, "look at me."

Cascabela lifted their head again. Their two working fists were curled at their sides.

"We've all lost friends," Barghest said—knowing, feeling, how inadequate the words were, and knowing that they had to be said anyway. "It's never easy."

"Of course not." Cascabela's voice was wooden. "But you can always make new friends on the front lines."

Barghest tried to gentle their voice. "I know you and Aconite were closer than most."

Cascabela didn't answer, but Barghest heard the grind of metal as their fists clenched tighter.

It wasn't at all like the crunch of a spear going through armor, but the noise still echoed in Barghest's ears. It didn't matter. "I won't tell you not to feel what you're feeling. Nothing should take that from you. But—"

"Everything gets taken from you, sir," said Cascabela. "Don't you know that by now?"

"*Cascabela.*"

"Sir!" Cascabela's arm swung into an impeccable salute. "Apologies for interrupting a superior officer, sir!"

They waited, parade straight, arm up, immobile as a statue. They had been doing this as long as Barghest, and they knew all the same tricks. Clearly they didn't intend to give an inch, but still Barghest had to try. "Cascabela—"

"Sergeant!"

"We're not done here," Barghest told Cascabela, and then headed towards Asher's call.

Asher stood up as they approached. "Dirk and Tvell need our help. While we were underground, they slid into a crack in the ice. They've been trapped there for—" She rubbed her face with her hands. "It must have happened while we were fighting the hyenas? I didn't check in with them at my usual time, and they—"

"You said they need our help," Barghest interrupted her. It was no more appropriate than Cascabela interrupting them earlier, but they knew the start of a spiral when they saw one. "They're both still alive?"

"Yes—yes." Barghest traced a small gesture of thanks to the gods, as Asher went on: "But Tvell's foot is caught, and Dirk can't pull them out by themself. I think, from where we are, we could—some of us could reach them? But it's hours out of the way, backtracking, and it's steep, and Svanik—"

"If I have to hear someone say 'and Svanik' in that tone of voice one more time," said Svanik, "I'm going to throw myself off this mountain right now."

Firzen slammed a hand, red with hyena blood, down into the snow. "You *can't* climb a mountain right now, Svanik!"

"I *know*!" The snap of Svanik's voice turned into a sharp cough, and they had to catch their breath before they went on. "Help them, leave me here. It's not a hard choice."

"Nobody's being left alone," said Asher, too loudly, then took a breath and re-pitched her voice. "And—it would be a hard climb for me, too. I'd slow you down."

"So you want to leave them," said Cascabela. Their voice boomed too loudly for someone who was only a foot away. "After all those fancy words."

"I really don't. But a small group would go faster. I think—" She glanced, for some reason, at Titan. "—maybe we should divide?"

"Divide," Barghest echoed.

Uneasily, they surveyed the group. There were already

too few of them for comfort. Five mostly functional Dedicates, plus Svanik and Asher: if another Levastan attack came, it wouldn't be enough. Even another pack of hyenas might be difficult to fend off.

They didn't want to leave Tvell and Dirk without help, but Asher's safety had to be their first priority. They met Asher's gaze, hoping she would see their doubts, but when she spoke, her voice sounded surer than before. "Barghest—you'll lead the rescue expedition. I'll stay here with Svanik."

"Sir," said Barghest, "you're the only one who can communicate with all of us." It was the closest they could come to reminding her that she should think of her own survival as something more than self-interest.

"I remember, Sergeant," answered Asher. "I wasn't going to suggest that the two of us stay alone." Her gaze ranged conscientiously back and forth over the Dedicates before settling. "Titan, will you stay with us? You're the least injured, I think."

"Probably," agreed Titan. "I don't mind."

Asher looked at Barghest. "You still don't like it, Sergeant."

So she was learning to read them, after all. "I agree," Barghest said, slowly, "that we should send a rescue party. But one or two others should suffice to assist them. I'd recommend that Titan and perhaps Dreizen—"

"I'll go," said Cascabela, still booming. "I'll go by myself if I have to."

"I said no one should be alone?" said Asher, too loud again. "I appreciate the recommendations, Sergeant— and that you volunteered, Cascabela. But there's safety in numbers, too, and if we've got to separate, I would feel better knowing that—um, I think there should probably be an officer in charge of each party? That's standard protocol, isn't it?"

Standard protocol couldn't always cover non-standard situations. But Barghest didn't say that. These past few days, when Asher had deferred to them out of inexperience—that wasn't standard protocol, either. It was her right to reassert the chain of command. They lifted a hand and saluted their acquiescence.

"Can I stay, too?" Firzen said.

Barghest and Asher both turned to look at them.

"I—if it's going to be hours anyway—" Firzen's lower hands fidgeted together. "There might be something I could do for Svanik? Now that we're outside and have the light, I want to at least take a better look."

"That seems reasonable," said Barghest, immediately. It didn't seem likely that much more could be done for Svanik without a field hospital, but they'd rather have one more Dedicate in fighting condition by Asher's side.

Asher hesitated a moment before nodding. "All right. Firzen, Titan, Svanik—you'll stay here. Barghest, Dreizen, and Cascabela will go on the mission. If you're lucky, you can get there and back before it gets too dark—but you'd better go now? While the weather holds. I'll be in touch with all of you, and—" She lifted her chin, her hand in the pocket that held the command plate. "And I'll see you all soon."

ASHER DIDN'T KNOW how long she'd been looking down the mountain when she heard footsteps coming towards her. She didn't look up. She knew who it had to be.

Titan came to stand on the ledge next to her. "You don't like listening to them either?"

Firzen and Svanik had been arguing since the others left—increasingly petty arguments, punctuated by long stretches of taut silence as Firzen's head swiveled between Svanik's injury and the damp pages of their medical text.

"It's hard," Asher said, to the skyline. She'd gotten used to the way her voice bounced back at her in the caves. Out here, the vastness of the sky seemed to swallow it up. "They're both so scared."

"Well, unfortunately," said Titan, "neither of them are stupid." They nudged a pebble absently with their foot. Asher watched it roll slowly towards the edge and winced, thinking of avalanches; Titan glanced at her, and then trapped it with their foot before it could go over. "How far are we from the rest of the army, do you think?"

"Not very far? A day to get off Green Adam, maybe, and two more on the path from there." Her gaze slid from the pebble trapped under Titan's foot, following the spur down which they would travel until it leveled off into tree cover. It didn't look anything like the thick line on the map she had memorized, but when she laid it down in her mind, sepia parchment over a jagged expanse of green, she was certain it matched. "It might be soon enough."

She'd done her best not to put a question in the words, but Titan answered anyway: "I'm gonna hope Firzen can figure out something to do for them here."

"That too," said Asher, and closed her eyes.

There was something she had to say; there would be no better time to say it. She'd sent Barghest away with the others so that she could.

"The chip in your control plate," she said, "it doesn't work, does it?"

She heard metal clanking against itself: Titan, tensing in surprise.

But they didn't respond, and so she knew she was right.

She looked at them, finally. At the empty spot on their wrist where Barghest had a dragon, and Cascabela had a death's-head, and Svanik and Dreizen and Firzen had nothing because their squad was new, and had not settled on a symbol yet. At the thin slits of their faceplate, behind which there was a person who always seemed to be watching her. Who noticed, more than any of the others, even Barghest, her small human expressions; who reacted to her grimaces. Her smiles.

"Is this some kind of test? Are you supposed to be watching, to see how I do?"

"What?" said Titan, unfeigned surprise in their voice. "They do that?"

"Not that I've ever heard, but I thought, maybe—" In many ways it would have been the easiest explanation. She knew how to pass tests. She swallowed, her voice lowering further. "Is—is it broken, then? Your chip, I mean? Did it stop working, or did you find a way to— Barghest doesn't know, do they? I'm sure they don't. Titan, I don't want to—if you did it yourself, I won't—"

But even as she spoke, she could feel how wrong the words felt, how the answer was not coming together the way that it should. Titan was not *reacting* the way they should. They had no reason to believe her, but they'd never been shy about challenging her before. If they were silent, it wasn't because they were afraid.

The immobile face was turned towards her, still. Nothing had changed. The darkness behind their grille was as impenetrable as ever.

In the caves, their iron arms had made her feel safe.

She took an involuntary step backwards, and said, stupidly, "But you *saved* me."

"Asher," Titan said—more gently than she'd ever heard them speak—"I didn't know the way off the mountain."

Then they lunged for her.

Asher scrambled backwards and screamed for Firzen, as Titan locked their metal hand around her forearm and swung her in a circle. She had just time to remember the crocuta that she had pulled off Cascabela before her head hit the rock of Green Adam.

HER BODY DANGLED limply from my hand, but Firzen was coming and I didn't have time to think about that. I held her up with one arm and shoved another hand into her pocket for the control plate.

I'd seen her do this at least four times now. As Firzen charged towards me, I looked at the plate, found their name, and put my hand on their chip.

"*Stop!*" I shouted—

—and "*Stop!*" I heard back, and thought for a moment that it was just an echo bouncing off the mountainside—

But it didn't sound like me; it sounded like Firzen, because I'd said it with their mouth. Theirs, as well as mine.

I'd known, but I hadn't *known*.

I stood, frozen, and so did they. I stared at myself through their eyes: a hulking armored monster swinging an unconscious girl, like one of Levasta's own army recruitment posters. Firzen's mind was a frightened itch scrabbling against mine, their voice trying to form words: *Titan, what's going on? What did you do? Is she dead?*

Then a different voice rasped into my ears: "What the *fuck*, Titan?"

I'd completely forgotten about Svanik. I moved my hand to cover their name on the plate, feeling Firzen's hand shift too as I did it, and then I was in three places at once, seeing the world from three different angles, and had to shut everybody's eyes at once to stop my head from spinning. Or maybe that was just Svanik—there was a wrongness in their body that I could feel, a sick dizziness so overwhelming that I could hardly believe they were standing on their own at all.

That didn't stop them from battering furious subvocalized questions at me. Firzen was doing the same, so fast I could hardly differentiate between them. "Shut up!" I snapped. It echoed across the mountain, in three different voices. "Give me a moment here!"

Silence fell immediately in my head—pressurized silence, like the heaviness that comes with a storm. I resisted the urge to put a hand to my head. I knew three hands would lift if I did.

When we were little, and undergoing the first of the procedures that would turn us into Dedicates, they'd talked our ears off about the glory of abdication and the holy altruism of self-surrender. Probably at some point they would have gotten more specific.

If Svanik got worse, if they passed out, could I make their body move anyway? Could I walk them all the way to Levasta?

I took a breath, feeling sicker than ever. "Svanik, you should be resting, or something. Go back and lie down." Three voices, including Svanik's, like the chorus in a play—but at least it helped obscure the panic in my own. I hadn't been ready for any of this. "Firzen, you can... you should just help them. Take care of them and leave me alone!"

They both hated it—I could feel them hating it—but they went, both of them, and I focused on opening a single set of eyes. Then, finally, I could turn my attention to Asher. I set her down carefully on the ground and checked her pulse.

The fluttering against my fingers made my stomach jump with a combination of relief and panic. I still didn't know how to get down the mountain. The last thing she'd done before I attacked her was try to do me a favor. I wasn't ready to have killed her yet.

If I *had* killed her, at least it would be over with—but I wasn't going to think about that now.

I picked her up again and carried her back to where I'd sent Firzen and Svanik. It had become extremely clear to me in the last three minutes that I didn't understand enough about the command plate to trust them out of my sight for long. Still, it seemed like giving them orders had more or less worked: Svanik was back on the ground, with Firzen kneeling next to them. Keeping them both in the corner of my eye, I knelt down and tied Asher up with a rope I'd been keeping in my lower left arm. She stirred a little as I pulled the rope taut, but didn't open her eyes or protest when I laid her against the cliffside.

All the while there was absolute silence from Firzen and Svanik. I'd gotten so used to hearing them bicker, I'd almost forgotten it was possible for them to be so quiet. They might as well have been dead.

I said, "Go ahead and talk if you want."

After a moment, Firzen burst out, "Why are you *doing* this?"

When I turned around to answer them, I saw that their medical book was trembling in their hands.

In Levasta, almost everyone I met was afraid of me.

I'd gotten used to that. Only just now did I realize how different it had felt, over the last week, not to carry that weight. For the first time in years, I'd just been one among many.

It hadn't been worth what Cesteli would have taken from me if I'd stayed. Nothing could be. Still, I wished I hadn't realized that it mattered that I'd missed that feeling, or that it hurt to lose it again. It was a fucking scam how the cost of my freedom kept going up.

I stood up and turned away from them. "Chat if you want," I said, loudly, "but don't go anywhere near the novice, understood? She stays right where she is. I'll be back."

I could feel their eyes boring into my back until I rounded the corner, back to that overhang where I'd attacked Asher, and got safely out of their sight.

Then I let myself drop to the ground. I put my head in my hands, the edge of the command plate a pressure against my forehead.

The next part was going to be worse.

"I CAN'T BELIEVE you found us!" Tvell said, for the third time. They had attached themself to Dreizen so firmly that their left arms might as well have been welded to Dreizen's back. If Asher or another commander had been present, Barghest might have discouraged this. "I really thought we'd never see you all again!"

"This one," said Dirk dryly, "has been nothing but laughs." Cascabela let out a snort.

"I thought I going to die in that crevice," said Tvell. "Ignominious starving doom. I really can't believe you found us!"

"*I* can't believe how little confidence you had in us," said Dreizen, and gave Tvell an affectionate knock. "Honestly, it's a little hurtful."

Barghest surveyed the group and fought the temptation to relax. They'd been lucky. The terrain hadn't been as difficult as they feared—or maybe it was just that the skies remained clear, and everything seemed a little easier with the sun bright overhead. Even Cascabela hadn't had much trouble on the climb, with their two remaining arms and Dreizen's assistance.

Still, the mountain could turn treacherous in an instant, and they would be slower on the return journey. Dirk was still weak from their earlier injuries, and though Tvell claimed to be able to walk on their own, Barghest was wary of pushing them too hard. They would still need luck to make it back to the others before dark.

They raised their voice. "All right, another hundred-count to rest, and then it's back down again. I'll want you spotting each other in pairs. Dirk and—"

Barghest's throat spasmed suddenly with the overlay of another presence. "Barghest?" they said, without volition. "Barghest?"

Inwardly, Barghest went very still. New commanders, promoted in a hurry or without proper training, didn't always know how to subvocalize when communicating through the command plate, but Asher seemed to have picked it up quickly. As they went up the mountain, her presence had been quiet and professional, a whisper that brushed the back of Barghest's throat so lightly it felt like mind-reading. There did not seem to be any reason that she would have forgotten those skills now.

Sir, Barghest acknowledged, cautiously—being very careful to subvocalize, hoping to set an example.

Whatever was happening, they didn't want to broadcast it to the entire unit. *Our mission's been successful. Is everything all right?*

Oh—that's how it works, said the person in their head. *Don't say anything. Just stay still. I'm sure you know by now this isn't your novice.*

The command was to stay still, so Barghest did. The command was not to say anything, so Barghest didn't. They did what they could do: deliberately ignored all their training, their carefully cultivated habits, and locked their muscles, knees, elbows, and gears down as tightly as they could. Stiff limbs were difficult to move, easy to over-balance.

It was never pleasant to be moved by someone else's will. You learned how to make it easier. If you survived long enough, you learned how to make it harder, too.

You said your mission was successful, right? the voice in the back of their throat whispered. *You got Tvell and Dirk?*

Barghest wondered, coldly, how long it would take the person to remember that they'd ordered Barghest not to say anything, and how literally that could be interpreted. The person. Not Asher, but someone who knew their mission, knew their names. Svanik, Firzen, or—

Answer me like this, just don't say anything to the others yet.

Barghest had already told them the mission was a success. A lie would be seen through easily. *Yes. Who is this? What's happened?*

Titan, said the person in their head, *but we're done with that now, so you might as well call me by my real name. It's Ester.*

I don't care, Barghest answered.

And immediately regretted it, in the sharp silence that followed. Instinct, when hurt, was to inflict answering hurt in whatever way was possible. But instinct was childish, and did not take the long view. As always, Barghest could not afford their own anger. They could not afford to lash out; there were others relying on them who needed all the information they could get. *What's happened to the others? The Commander?*

For a moment they thought that Titan—Ester—wasn't going to answer. Then Ester said, *Everyone's all right for now. Dirk and Tvell? Can they walk?*

If Barghest lied, Ester might force Barghest to abandon them. *They can walk.*

Good. Don't climb back down to us. Keep on the way you're going. You're going to lead them all to the other side of the mountain, and then, said Ester, who was not and had never been Titan, *you're all going to turn towards the east. Towards the Levastan border.*

To Levasta, echoed Barghest. *Why?*

To fight for them. Ester's answer rose like bile in the back of their throat. *To train with them, to be studied by them. To help them win the war.*

Barghest stopped breathing, as if they could shut off the words that way, but Ester continued, inexorable. *I came here to steal you, Barghest. I'm sorry—I really am sorry—but you're a Levastan asset now.*

Barghest couldn't speak, couldn't yell. Through their peripheral vision, they could see the others looking at them in concern. Their chest pounded with the air they could not use to shout with.

I really am sorry, Ester said again, after another moment. *But you're a weapon either way, and I can't let you be Cesteli's. Don't you see?*

Barghest forced themself to exhale. To breathe, in and out.

Look—Barghest—look. Listen. There's no way Levasta doesn't win this in the end. They're five times Cesteli's size. They've got the money and the numbers. The faster it ends, the better for everyone.

Barghest's hands were shaking. Was that them or was that Ester?

Once it's over, nobody else will have to be Dedicated, nobody else will have to die—come on! You've dragged this out so long, and for what? You and me, everyone here, we're already casualties! What's so special about Cesteli that you have to keep this up no matter how many kids it costs?

It would do no good to get angry. It never did any good.

Barghest had only been two years old when the first invasion happened. They didn't remember the soldiers, or the deaths of their parents, or the victory parades when Cesteli's standing army had halted the advance of what—in ever-perfect hindsight—had obviously only been a preliminary feint. A test of Cesteli's strength, to see how many resources Levasta should commit towards the task of re-incorporating its splintered-off heretic sister.

They didn't remember being brought to the Holiest House in Linnea, but they remembered Sor Zarra's lessons in theology, Sor Carmel's classes on astronomy, and Sor Annata's tutorials in sewing, how patient she had been as they tried to match the impossible precision of her clockwork hands. Sor Zusa's irritable frown at being pulled from her research; Sor Josanna's kindness as her soft-piped voice soothed them through nightmares. The sisters of the Holiest Houses, as they had been before the war.

And they remembered, better than all of that, the second invasion: the soft-bodied sisters hurrying all of their wards out of the Holiest House, while the habited lined up behind them to buy them time.

Later, they'd all sat on a high ridge, safe behind army lines, and watched the enormous bonfire the Levastan troops had built in the courtyard of the sanctuary. The melting copper in the lost sisters' habits had turned the flames a brilliant blue-green that Barghest had never seen before. They'd seen it many times since.

"We should have been the ones to stay," they remembered Sor Zarra saying, her voice choked and thick. "We should have let them take the children, and defended the place in their stead. It's the habited ones they really hate. For us, there might have been mercy."

And Sor Zusa had answered: "Probably not."

Barghest?

Some time after that, at the Holiest House in Rosavera—well behind the lines, and packed full of refugees—Sor Zarra had come and gathered all the war-orphans around her. Her face had been wet and prickly. It was the last time Barghest could remember seeing her human face. She'd taken the habit not long afterwards.

She'd hugged them all, and then she had told them that the governing council and the heads of the church had come to a difficult decision. Cesteli's Holiest Houses could not keep orphans anymore, as they had done for hundreds of years. There were too many, and with so many border Houses burned, there was not room or food enough for them all. Only very special children could stay; only very brave children; only children who would never have an apprenticeship, or a family, or anything but service to their country and the gods.

Those children who chose to stay would be made strong, so that they could protect the weak. For all the rest, they would find what places they could.

"I want you to remember," Sor Zarra had said to them—and Barghest had remembered, had gone on remembering, every day of the eighteen years since—"that there are other futures you could have. You've got—oh, holy skies!" She'd hidden her face in her hands, and all of them had exchanged nervous glances, afraid she would start crying again; there was nothing that made you feel more helpless than an adult who cried. But her shoulders had only shaken once, and then she'd straightened, and put her arms around the children to either side of her. "If you stay, you must do it selflessly. Not because you're afraid to leave. Not even because you love us, or because we love you. There will be other people out there to love you, and staying will be more frightening than going. If you stay, you'll be giving yourself, like the habited sisters did when they saved us, and you'll have no reward for it in this world any more than they did. Do you understand?"

Barghest had been seven years old, then, and their name had not yet been Barghest. Of course they had not understood.

They had chosen, all the same.

Barghest, you need to get the others moving!

They used different words, now, in the Holiest House. Nobody told the children who were Dedicated these days that there were other lives they could have. What would be the point? The army needed the Dedicates too badly. There were too many war-orphans, and nowhere else for them to go.

Levasta kept on coming. It would not stop until it had taken everything that made them different from itself, everything that made them Cesteli. Already the younger ones—novices and Dedicates—didn't know what had been lost.

But Barghest had been among the first, and Barghest remembered.

This is an order! Barghest!

"Start moving," murmured Barghest obediently, and then did nothing.

They went on doing nothing, their limbs heavy and uncooperative, as they felt their body hauled around, like a puppet's; as their knees knocked awkwardly together; as their voice declared, in desperate tones that were not their own, "Everybody, listen up. We've got new orders now. We're going a different way."

Dreizen and Tvell stared at each other, horror written in the line of their shoulders. Dirk looked off to the side, as Barghest had often done themself to spare a comrade the indignity of spectacle.

But Cascabela met their gaze dead-on, and held it until Barghest felt their eyes jerked away and upwards, towards the washed-out blue sky. A gray wall of cloud was rolling in. It looked like it would soon begin again to snow.

ONCE AGAIN ASHER woke up to pain, and snowflakes, and Dedicates talking in the background.

"—if I make like I'm dying *right now*, maybe—"

"You really think there's any chance they'll fall for that?"

Svanik, she identified, with profound relief, and Firzen.

She tried to reach her hand to her forehead, but something prevented her from doing so. She was bound. She was lying on the ground, tied at the wrists and ankles. This, at least, was new.

She was alive, which, when she finally managed to review the last few events in her memory, came as something of a surprise.

She opened her eyes. Svanik was croaking, "It might at least distract Titan for—"

"She's awake!" Firzen interrupted. "Sir, are you all right?" They sounded glad, Asher realized, with another gulp of relief. Of course there was no *particular* reason she should expect anything else, but after Titan—

Belatedly, she registered the worried silence at the fact that she had not answered yet. "I'm—all right, I think? I don't think anything's—um, are you? All right?"

"We're not worse than we were, but—sir, I'm so sorry, they've got the command plate and they said we can't untie you, or even go near you—"

"It's all right," Asher said, hastily. "I understand." She tried to lever herself up to a sitting position without the use of her hands. The pounding in her head intensified as the angle of her neck shifted, but after a few moments she could look more or less directly at Firzen. "Um—did they say anything about why—what they wanted? What their plans were?"

"Just a lot of flaming *shit*!" said Firzen, fiercely, and then ducked their head, embarrassed. A bubble of maybe-hysterical laughter rose in Asher's throat. She didn't think she'd ever heard Firzen curse before. "Ah—I mean, nothing useful, sir."

"Ah," said Asher. "That's too bad." The words sounded inane as soon as she heard them out loud. "Um, I mean, if we at least knew who they really were—"

Svanik said, "What do you mean, who?"

"Oh," said Asher. "That's why they—their command chip doesn't—I don't think they're a real Dedicate?"

"Depends how you define it," said Titan.

Asher swung her torso around so fast she almost fell back over again.

Titan stood on the precipice of the plateau, holding the command plate. Their hands were shaking in a way that Asher didn't like—but then again, perhaps she shouldn't be unhappy to see shaky hands on a person who had very recently swung her head into a rock.

It was surprisingly difficult. She did not seem to have found the space to be angry yet. Surely it would come soon; surely she was not pathetic enough that she could only be sad, and nothing else.

"How do you," she asked, and was embarrassed all over again by the weak wobbling of her own voice, "define it?"

Titan stepped towards her. Asher consciously resisted the urge to flinch backwards, but they must have seen something on her face anyway. They halted, looking down at her from what seemed like miles up. "In Levasta," they said, conversationally enough, "they say Dedicates are monsters whose souls have been stolen by blood magic. I didn't actually think they were wrong."

"You were in Levasta?" said Firzen, startled, but Titan went on without acknowledging them.

"When they put the godstone in the base of my neck, I didn't know what to be scared of. I was just as brainwashed then as anyone. Then, later, I thought I'd just gotten lucky, to have escaped before—before whatever the final step had to be. Before everything that made me a person got crushed up and left on the altar of your stupid gods of sacrifice. You took my name and my face, and that was bad enough, but I thought I still had something left that the others didn't, that made me not—like them." Their voice cracked; their head turned in the direction of Firzen and Svanik, and then back towards Asher. "I thought that for a long time."

They suddenly crouched down next to Asher, alarmingly large, alarmingly close. "I was wrong. You don't steal anybody's souls. You steal our bodies, and we can *feel* it—" They held the command plate up. "I think that might be worse."

Their hands were still shaking. Asher wanted to grab one to make it stop.

"You really were Dedicated," she whispered. She'd never heard of a Dedicate outside the army, out from under the aegis of the Holiest Houses. "Were you—did Levasta kidnap you, or—"

"*You* kidnapped me," said Titan, flatly. "You—your Holiest Houses, your sisters, your gods—you took me, like you do all the other kids nobody wants, and you turned me into a monster."

"You're not a monster," protested Asher, without thinking.

She heard one of the Dedicates behind her snort, but Titan's head stayed turned towards her. "No?" they said, after a long moment. "Nice of you to say under the circumstances. But I don't know that it means much coming from you."

They leaned a little closer. She couldn't smell anything but iron. "I thought that you—that you were harmless, sort of. That you meant well, or thought you did. Then I tried doing what you do." They brandished the command plate in front of her face. "You do this all the time—nobody should do this to another person, *ever*, and you just—do it! All the time! Did you ever even think about it?"

Through the haze of fear, Asher wanted to protest that she had, she *had* thought about it. She'd been assigned dozens of tracts and commentaries discussing the moral implications of actions undertaken while subsumed under another's will. Sor-philosophers debated it constantly.

But that wasn't what Titan was talking about.

She knew what they were talking about. She'd felt it each time she'd used the command plate—Tvell's stiff limbs, when she'd almost overbalanced them on the mountain; Cascabela's silent resistance in their compliance—and each time she'd fled back to her body, and shoved her discomfort into the back of her mind.

She hadn't had time to think about it. It wasn't her duty to think about it. She wasn't a general or a soteriologist or a theological scientist, just a novice plunged into a situation well over her head. It shouldn't even have been her duty to get them all off the mountain, and now that it *was* her duty, it was taking everything she had to accomplish it.

And once she *had* gotten everyone off the mountain— once she had brought all her Dedicates back to the army, to which they belonged—would she have thought about it again?

When she returned to her responsibilities, and was given more of them—when she rose in the ranks, as she expected she might—when she had a path to follow, and things that were expected of her, and people to look to for approval who were not the soldiers that surrounded her—would she ever have thought about it?

She didn't know.

But she also knew that she still didn't have the time to think about it now, not the way she needed to think about it. They weren't off the mountain yet.

She took a deep breath, and said, "If you don't want to use the command plate then... then maybe you just shouldn't?"

She'd meant it to come out with bravado and spirit; in fact it sounded thin, weak, and childish. The mask of Titan's face seemed to radiate scorn. "Oh?" they said. She couldn't decipher their tone. "So?"

Asher swallowed. Behind the iron grille there was a person who could be reasoned with, she *knew* that there was. She couldn't blame them for the horror in their voice when they talked about the command plate. They cared about the others, even if they didn't care about her.

"You can keep a sword at my neck or whatever you like, but—whatever you want, can't it wait? Barghest and the others are still out there—if you let me talk to them—if we can all just get somewhere safe—"

"You want it back." Titan's laugh had a jagged sound. "There's really nothing in there but Cesteli fucking gospel, is there?"

"No—" Asher struggled for words. "That's not—"

At the same time, Firzen spat, "You're a liar and a traitor, and you're questioning *her* morals?"

Titan didn't turn back towards Firzen. "I'm a Levastan citizen these days," they answered. "And I haven't betrayed my country yet."

They stood up, in a quick unsteady motion. "But I'd rather be a traitor than a slaver," they added, their voice suddenly strong, and then Titan took the command plate between all four of their hands, and broke it.

THE CRACK OF sound as the command plate shattered echoed louder in my ears than the avalanche had. Shards of godstone pattered down around my feet. I could feel my hands shaking, my knees knocking together, as Barghest's knees had knocked when I dragged their body around to give orders to the others. My body was more or less the same as theirs. We had all the same parts with all the same plating—the same human flesh underneath, godstone fucking resonant—only mine was *mine,* and theirs had been nothing but dead weight.

And now, having been in theirs, mine felt like dead weight, too. It would be a long time before I forgot it.

It would have been me. If it weren't for my mother, if it weren't for Levasta—it would have been me, trapped and helpless as somebody dragged me around from the inside.

Someone like Asher. She stared up at me, yellowing old bruises on one side of her face from the avalanche and new vivid purple ones on the other and a bright red stress zit blooming on her chin. Her bound hands clenched tightly together, and then she banged them down, hard, on my foot. "What have you *done?*"

Of course it didn't hurt, but it startled me so much I almost jumped anyway. "Are you in a position to piss me off?" I spat.

"You just cut Barghest off from—they were counting on me for directions! What if they can't remember the way back to us?" She was so agitated that she was hardly hesitating over her words at all. "Titan, when you were using the command plate, what did you tell them to do? Where did you send them? It's starting to snow again!"

I stared at her, frozen, trying to think—

And then I heard a sound behind me, and I snatched Asher up again from the ground, two arms to hold her and a metal hand around her throat.

I spun around towards Firzen. "You want to take another step?" I demanded. My voice was high-pitched and harsh in my own ears. They thought I was a killer—I sounded like one—I'd planned to be one—so all right. "I could snap her neck easily. I don't need a command plate for that."

All four of Firzen's fists balled at their sides.

"Honestly," I said—to Firzen, and to Svanik behind them—"I don't even particularly want to. But if you *did* take that step—" Asher's throat bobbed under my hand as she swallowed. "—if you decided you hated me enough to risk her life, I guess I'd be impressed. You're free now, right? Do whatever you want."

Then I threw Asher at Firzen and fled down the mountain.

THE IMPACT KNOCKED the breath out of her. She clutched instinctively at Firzen as they staggered backwards, and had a sudden disorienting flashback to Tvell teetering at the edge of the cliff face.

"Sir," Firzen gasped, "are you all right?"

Asher wished, with all her heart, that they didn't have to ask her that so often. "Yes, I'm—"

"I'm going to catch them," said Svanik, and surged to their feet.

"Svanik, *sit down!*" Asher shouted, and heard Firzen's roar echoing the same words, their carapace vibrating with the force of it.

"Make me," Svanik suggested, almost gleefully—took several running steps past them towards the cliff edge where Titan had fled—and then, abruptly, dissolved into a coughing fit so violent that they lost their balance and fell to the ground.

Firzen stared. Then: "I hate them," they said, with passion. "I hate them *so much*." For a moment Asher was not sure whether they were talking about Titan or Svanik, before they added, "They're going to kill themself!" and launched themself after Svanik.

"At least they didn't get far?" said Asher. She felt nauseous from the motion of Firzen's running, or perhaps from the second head injury in a week, or both. "Um. You could put me down."

Firzen startled, then stopped long enough to set her carefully on the ground before dropping to their knees next to Svanik. "I'm sorry, sir, I just—"

"I know," said Asher. Her hands and feet were still tied, but this did not seem the most important thing to mention when Svanik was still prone on the ground. "Are—are they—"

"I'm not dead yet," growled Svanik.

Asher jumped; Firzen didn't. "You shouldn't talk," they snapped, and went on with their inspection. "Try acting like you want to recover! For once!"

"Someone had to go after them," croaked Svanik. "Did you—"

They dissolved into another coughing fit, and Firzen turned to give Asher what would probably have been a look of despair if they had a face to give it with. "Can you order them to stop?"

Svanik made a phlegmy sound that might have been a laugh. "Orders don't matter now, do they? Just my luck—" They choked, then banged on their chest plate and went on as if nothing had happened—"when I'm like *this*—"

"Svanik," said Firzen, "*please*, stop, just *breathe*—"

"This is important!" insisted Svanik, and struggled up

to a sitting position. "Didn't you see? They were holding the command plate—they might still have some of it—"

"It's all right," Asher said, as soothingly as she could. "It's destroyed. They can't do anything with it."

"They can bring it to Levasta, can't they? They said—" Asher wanted to cover her ears against the harsh sound of Svanik's breathing as they struggled to get the words out. "They said they're Levastani, what if they bring it *back* there, and Levasta figures out—"

"I don't think—" Asher began, but cut herself off. "No. You're right."

She wanted to think that Titan wouldn't do such a thing. That they wouldn't want Levasta to learn the secrets of how Cesteli used godstone; that they'd meant it when they said they would rather be a traitor than a slaver.

She wanted to think that, but it was very clear that she had no way to make an objective judgment on the topic. Titan had been upset, and their hands had been shaking. She'd thought they were sincere. But she didn't *know*. Once their head cleared and they got themself under control, they might decide to do anything.

What *could* Levasta do, with a double handful of broken godstone?

"You're right," she said again, and swallowed. "But there's—I don't know that there's anything we can do about it? We won't catch them now, and we can't split up more, when we don't even know where Barghest—" To her horror, her own voice wobbled in a way that presaged tears. She absolutely couldn't cry in front of Firzen and Svanik. She could *not*. She swallowed it all down, and forced herself to go on. "Barghest and the others are still out there. Maybe they'll see Titan, and—"

As she said it, she knew how ridiculous it was. She carried a map of the mountain in her head. There was no way to imagine that any two people, wandering in vaguely the same direction, in a *snowstorm,* would encounter each other by surprise. Still: "Right," said Firzen, stoutly attempting to back her lead. "The Sergeant will take care of it."

"The Sergeant doesn't know!" Svanik snapped. "The Sergeant's been commanded—"

"But the command plate's broken!" said Asher. For the first time, it felt like a relief. "They won't have to follow whatever Titan's orders were anymore, they—they can just come back the way they came."

"They don't *know* though," said Svanik, again, and Asher felt the hope that had flared up in her die away.

"You mean—because the order was given before the command plate was broken, they'll still have to...?"

"We don't know," Firzen said, in a voice that sounded suddenly very young. "Nothing like this has ever happened before."

"Or if it has," rasped Svanik, "they wouldn't tell *us.*"

Silence fell heavier than the snow. Asher drew in a breath, and reached, once again, for her commander-voice. Her responsibilities had not dissolved with the command plate. Nothing was ever that easy. "Well— either way, there's nothing we can do about that right now, so we'd better find shelter while the storm passes? Luckily, we never got a chance to move away from the cave, so..."

"Luckily," muttered Svanik, with intense sarcasm.

"Svanik," said Asher, "*please* be quiet, there's really nothing else you have to say that's important—"

Important enough to risk your health for, she'd meant to say, but she was interrupted by Firzen's giggling. It was, possibly, hysterical. It was also probably unkind to Svanik. Still: "That's an order," Asher said instead, watching Firzen's shoulders shake with laughter, and felt again, with surprise, that sense of relief where the weight of the command plate should have been. She could give an order, and an order was all it was. It didn't have to be anything else.

And if Svanik's silence had a certain mutinous quality to it, it wasn't compelled, either.

She turned to Firzen. "Um—if you'll untie me, I can help you bring them into the cave—"

"Holy *skies!*" Firzen had apparently used up their allotment of real expletives; now they sounded like somebody's elderly aunt. Asher swallowed back a giggle as hysterical as theirs had been. "You're still tied up? Sir, I'm so—"

"It's all right," said Asher. "There's been, um. A lot."

Firzen untied her, and together they helped Svanik back over the rocky incline that led into the caves. "I'll leave something bright-colored," said Asher, "so it will be easy for the others to spot us, if—if they're coming this way." Though perhaps it was a bad idea to put out something conspicuous enough that an enemy troop could see it. Barghest would be annoyed that she'd taken the risk. Or, maybe not annoyed—Barghest never seemed to let themself get annoyed—but polite in the way that meant they were tired and disappointed.

She wouldn't mind Barghest being disappointed in her, so long as they were *here*. Asher climbed back outside, bringing blue stockings with her.

As she squinted through the falling snow for a place to tie the stockings, her eye caught something on the ground, gray and glimmering with frost.

It was a piece of the command plate.

For a moment, she was tempted to leave it there. It would only be an hour or so until the snow covered all the pieces up, and who else would come across them, all the way up here? Who else would even know what they were? And what else was she going to do—carry the shards all the way back to the army as evidence of how badly she'd done, and how much she'd failed?

Though of course there was still the matter of the Dedicates' sympathetic chips. The plate was broken, but perhaps not all the chips were. The Dedicates could be assigned to new units, their markers put into other plates—

Her train of thought stopped there, caught on the remembered scorn in Titan's voice. Her mind felt like the gears in Sor Elena's habit had sounded after the spear pierced them.

She bent and picked up the broken piece of godstone. The jagged edges snagged on the fabric of her gloves. There were two chips in it, still. Two serial numbers, now easily mapped to names.

Titan's chip, useless and false, next to Cascabela's.

She pulled her right hand out of its glove, hesitated, then set the pad of her finger down on Cascabela's chip. She was braced for a rush of sensation—they'd all been warned about the dangers of handling raw godstone— but instead an echo of emotion settled over her like a bad headache: an involuntary tension in the muscles of her arm, a bitter taste in her mouth. She strained for the thread that would let her drift away from her body and into Cascabela's, but it was too diffuse to follow. All she could tell was that, somewhere, far away from her, they were angry.

Well, she didn't need a chip to tell her that.

She pulled her hand away and put her glove back on, the bitterness lingering on her tongue. Why should she think Titan's chip was any more useless than Cascabela's? Without the amplification of the command plate, she couldn't reach them regardless.

She turned the shard over in her hands, as if looking at the other side could show her a solution. The gears of her mind were grinding back and forth again over the same thought they had snagged on before. Cascabela's chip was not useless. It was still sympathetic, still linked to the other half of itself embedded at the base of Cascabela's skull—a direct connection between body and soul.

Godstone could be unpredictable, but it was always soul-resonant.

It really was as the sisters had always said: the only thing you could truly control was yourself.

Asher shoved the shard into her pocket, then dropped to her knees, scrabbling at the snow. Here was Firzen's chip, whole; here dead Aconite's, broken—surely that couldn't be all? The shards had been dropped, not thrown, but then there had been the struggle... and what if Svanik was right, and Titan carried off some of the pieces? She took off her gloves and ran her hands over the ground, hunting by feel. Her robes grew soaked, her hands and knees scraped and numb.

When she found Barghest's chip—a whisper of weary despair under her fingers—she did cry, with relief. The tears were hot, and warmed her frozen cheeks.

Back in the cave, Firzen had propped Svanik up against a wall and was laying out surgical implements on a cloth. "I only have the little ones," they told her fretfully, without looking up. "From my arm storage.

The big ones were lost in the avalanche. These are all the wrong size for an amputation, even if—"

"What about for a smaller operation?" said Asher.

Firzen looked up at her. "What do you mean?"

Asher's hand tightened on Barghest's shard. The relief at finding it had passed; she felt cold and sick and scared.

She could still leave them. She could leave them all—leave Svanik, too; she and Firzen alone could not carry them—and bring Firzen with her back down the mountain, hoping that Barghest and the others would find their way to safety somehow.

But her duty was to get them all off the mountain. She had *promised* to get them all off the mountain.

She lifted up the shard and held it out to Firzen.

"The Sergeant's sympathetic chip," she said. "Could you put it where yours is?"

Firzen's hand drifted to the back of their head in confusion. "Um—"

"Sorry, I—that was unclear. I meant—" She put her own hand to the base of her neck, under her hair. The cold of her own half-frozen fingers burned into her skin. The First Texts said that the body was nothing, and sacrifice was sacred, and a selfless act of the soul let humans approach the gods, and if she couldn't at least act like she believed it then she shouldn't have ever picked up a command plate. "Where yours is, but on me. Where the body meets the soul? To connect us. Me and Barghest."

Firzen dropped the scalpel they were holding.

Then they picked it up again, with fumbling fingers. It was probably just as well that Asher couldn't see their face. "Sir, I've never—you're not a Dedicate, and I'm not—"

"I know," said Asher. Her voice sounded steady compared to theirs; it would have to do. "I don't know how it will work either. But it's that, or abandoning them, and I won't——"

She could still turn back. The shard was sharp in her hand. She didn't know what fate she was condemning either of them to, but Barghest was lost in the snow, and she'd made a promise.

She swallowed down her doubts, and went on: "I won't do that."

SNOW FELL IN sheets around them. They didn't know how long they had been marching. The world was cold and gray.

And then, suddenly, it was also a different kind of gray.

The back of their neck—it took Barghest several moments to remember that there was a word for the sharp sting of that sensation.

They were marching, still. They were marching, with Cascabela in front of them and Dreizen behind, and also they were lying down on their stomach, and it hurt. As the pain descended once more, they reared up and flung themselves around—

"Sir!" said Firzen's voice, frightened, and: "Sir!" cried Dreizen, as Barghest suddenly spun on their heel, kicking up a wheel of white.

They saw Dreizen. They saw Firzen. They felt the cold of the air on their skin, on *skin*—

And then they shut their eyes—*someone* shut their eyes—and they didn't see Firzen anymore, only Dreizen and the mountain and the falling snow.

Sorry! Sorry. I should have kept my eyes closed. It's easier when you're only seeing one thing at once.

It wasn't just a voice in the back of their throat. It was a voice in the back of their head.

Sir, Barghest subvocalized, deliberately, *may I call a halt?*

The answer came almost like a sob. *Please.*

"Halt!" Barghest shouted, their voice a loud snap in the frozen air.

And at the same time they felt themself say, in a soft strained voice, "Sorry, Firzen, I'll—I just need a few moments. I'm all right. It's like this because it worked."

There was another sensation on their back, distantly familiar, almost forgotten. Not just pain, but something warm and trickling.

We're bleeding, Barghest realized, and only understood that they'd formed it into a thought when Asher answered, *Yes.*

Barghest breathed in and out and in again. They would not be overwhelmed. They had their own familiar body, and they still had control of it. They arranged themself on a stable point safely away from the cliff edge, half-expecting at each moment to feel one of their muscles moved by Asher's will instead of their own; none were.

Then they closed their own eyes inside their visor.

And opened them in a cave with Firzen hovering anxiously nearby, a threaded needle in one hand.

"It's all right now," Asher said. Barghest felt the muscles of their mouth move as she aimed an expression at Firzen before turning to face the wall. "You can finish the stitches."

The pain bloomed again, but Barghest found that, if they tried, they could recede from it. Their own neck also had a back, and it didn't feel things the same way.

Yes—I don't think you have to be all the way here all the time?

Sir, Barghest thought, forming each word with care, *what have you done?*

They felt Asher suck in a gulp of air as Firzen's needle descended, and then do her best to answer the same way. *Titan broke the command plate.*

The wave of Barghest's shock must have run through both of them, because Asher's muscles tensed, and Firzen said, "Please don't move, sir!"

Sorry, thought Asher, and said, out loud, "Sorry."

Barghest kept their focus on breathing, and on thinking only and exactly what they meant to think. *That doesn't fit with their mission as they explained it to me.*

Something halfway between a sentence and an emotion spiked into their mind—*oh, you got an explanation?*—followed by a deliberate phrase: *Whatever their mission was, they seem to have had second thoughts.*

From the contrast, Barghest suspected that the first part was not something they had been meant to hear. They redoubled their efforts to keep the surface of their mind calm. *If they broke the command plate, then—*

"It's done," said Firzen, and Barghest realized that the jabbing at the back of their neck had stopped. The pain wasn't gone, just dimmed, one among another dozen small aches that flared and receded as Asher turned around again.

"Thank you," she said, to Firzen, and to Barghest, she thought: *I think we're—um, I have the other half of your chip. I'm sorry. I couldn't think of another way to reach you.*

Can it be undone?

I don't know. Are you upset?

It doesn't matter, Barghest answered; then, immediately overwhelmed by a wave of Asher's anxious guilt—she'd had to do it, she'd known they might hate it, she'd known they might hate her, what would she *do* if they hated her—amended their response. *No.*

She had prevented an unimaginable catastrophe. She had made a tactical decision, for the benefit of her troops. It was her decision to make as commander.

Anything else, everything else, Barghest could wait to process until they had better learned how to maintain the division between them and ensure that their thoughts stayed their own.

Asher's eyes were open now, but Barghest was learning how to keep her frame of vision at arm's length. In their own body, they saw the other Dedicates watching them warily, forms dimly visible through the falling snow.

Barghest lifted their voice. "We're turning around! We're going back to camp!"

The others all began talking at once; Barghest put up a hand to silence them. "You deserve answers, but it will have to wait until we're back. In weather like this, we can't afford any distractions."

The command plate was broken. They would all know about it eventually, but it couldn't be here, and it couldn't be now—not on a cliffside; not in a blizzard; not when Barghest had themself so little under their own control.

As they climbed back down, they became aware that the buzz of Asher's thoughts was dimming: she had curled herself up against the cave wall and was mumbling through repeats of a meditation mantra with her eyes closed and her hands over her ears. It was the best thing she could have done to minimize the risk that their doubling posed to Barghest's descent, and Barghest was grateful. There was no helping the way that her body's unfamiliar pain throbbed through Barghest with every step they took. Barghest did their best not to let her know they felt it.

After a while, they heard Firzen's muffled voice through Asher's ears: "Sorry to bother you, sir, but I thought you'd want to know—it looks like the snow's starting to stop."

The mental hum of meditation came to a halt. *That's not true yet where you are,* said Asher, to Barghest.

No.

I'm going to stand outside? I want to make sure you don't miss us.

Barghest immediately made their mind blank. They couldn't let Asher feel a wave of disapproval every time they disagreed with one of her decisions. They were attempting to frame a careful suggestion that Asher's attempt at sensory deprivation had been more helpful than her signposting when they felt her body shudder with an indrawn gasp.

Barghest!

Barghest had just enough presence of mind to bring their own body to stillness and shout for a halt before their focus narrowed on the figure that Asher had seen through the opening of the cave. A single Dedicate, balanced on a ledge not fifty feet away, looking down at the valley below.

A Dedicate with proper training wouldn't expose themself that way. They wouldn't assume there were no enemies around. But Ester, Barghest knew, had not had proper training, and this made them vulnerable.

A whisper of thought, from Asher: *They said they didn't know how to get off the mountain. I guess they got turned around in the snowstorm, and don't know which way to go? Or—they might not even know where they want to go?*

It was an insight that Barghest would likely not have come to on their own, but once Asher presented the idea, it felt inevitable. Where, indeed, could Ester want to go? They had betrayed their comrades for a mission, and then apparently thrown that mission away as well, on some kind of passing whim. There was nothing binding them to anywhere: no responsibilities, no loyalties, no ties to country or gods.

I think they have gods—a thought of Asher's so irrelevant to Barghest that it registered no more than the sting of Asher's fingernails biting into the skin of her palms as they clenched their fists. There was so much they couldn't be angry about, but there were limits. A person had limits.

They had thought they would never see Ester again. They had thought that what Ester had tried to do to them would be one more thing to live with, and move past.

And here Ester was like a miracle—the kind of miracle that Cesteli theologians said the gods did not deliver, because they were distant, up in the heavens, and could affect nothing.

Which was why they needed Dedicates to act for them.

YOU SAID THEY *might still have some shards of the command plate.* Barghest's thoughts were cold and sharp as stalactites, shattering through Asher's attempt to pull together a strategy. *We're going to get them back.*

How?

Let me.

She lifted her arm—*she* didn't lift her arm—*they* lifted her arm, Barghest deliberately lifted her arm, and all of

Asher's instincts screamed that she should struggle and push back, that her body was hers to use and hers alone.

If you do that, we won't succeed.

She wanted to nod. She wanted to breathe, a long, deep breath, and center herself once more. But that was exactly what she could not do, what she must not do.

If she couldn't give up control—as the Dedicates were asked to do every day—then she was nothing but the worst kind of hypocrite, and everything Ester had said about her was true.

She wasn't sure she'd ever been more frightened. She could feel the rage pouring off Barghest like sublimating ice. Her own thoughts seemed scattered and diffuse in the wake of their anger—but in spite of all that, Barghest remained Barghest. The kindness that was all they had ever let show was real too. *It's all right,* they told her. *It takes time for anyone to learn that balance. But—*

But we can't afford a mistake, she agreed. *I have to let you have control. I know.*

She knew, too, what Barghest was not allowing themself to consider: if Asher fought Barghest for control of her body, she was fairly sure she would lose.

That thought, she clamped down.

Should I get Firzen? she asked.

Ester will hear them coming. The first attack has to be us.

Her fear spiked again, heart pounding with adrenaline, followed by embarrassment. She knew that Barghest could feel both. *But they're a Dedicate, and I'm just—*

We'll take them by surprise, Barghest sent back, firm and reassuring. She could almost think they were moved only by logic, if it weren't for their anger still ringing in her ears. *We can do it, if you'll trust me.*

I trust you. It was the answer she knew they wanted.

And it was true. It had to be true. She was the one who had chosen this for both of them.

She let her arms go, and her back and shoulders and still-stinging neck, and stepped into a corner of herself to watch.

Impossibly, their internal discussion had only taken a few moments. Titan—no, Ester, Barghest had called them Ester—hadn't moved; Asher could feel Barghest's scorn at the fact that they were still standing there. Asher's body edged carefully backwards. Her limbs moved gingerly at first, then with more confidence. Barghest was learning what they were capable of.

Firzen looked up as she approached, and Asher's right hand moved in an unfamiliar arrangement. *Signal for silence,* Barghest told her, as they knelt down by Svanik.

Firzen's head swiveled to follow them as they went, but despite their clear shock, they didn't make a sound. Asher wondered if they understood just how well their surgery had worked. Barghest methodically unlatched Svanik's lower arm compartment, pulled out a long knife that was strapped to the inside, and closed it up again. Then they reached for the iron pot in which Firzen had been boiling water, and grabbed that too before returning to the cave entrance.

Asher felt the sharp surge of their relief as they saw that Ester was still there. Her heart—their heart—pounded. She didn't think they knew how much they were letting her see.

Keeping Asher's body low, Barghest crept through the slowing snow to the cliff edge down which Ester had jumped, an hour or two and a soul-change ago. They looked down at the drop, assessing, and then thoughtfully back up at the rock of the mountain, dotted with uneven heaps of new-fallen snow.

Then they pulled Asher's arm back and threw the cookpot towards Ester.

It wasn't as far or as hard a throw as they'd hoped; it was more than Asher herself would have thought her arm capable of. Asher felt a flash of their disappointment, but they were already leaping over the cliff, hitting a pile of snow six or seven feet below just as the cookpot banged against the ground near Ester's feet.

Ester whirled in the direction the cookpot had come from—where Asher had been just a moment ago—and meanwhile Barghest was moving Asher's body towards Ester as fast as it could go, heedless of the freezing pain in her hands and knees where they'd landed hard on snow-covered rock. Hearing their progress, Ester spun to catch them in their limited field of vision, but Barghest had already pulled Asher's body the other way in a movement that had seemed meaningless until Asher saw how Ester had to twist to see them coming. She could feel Barghest's surprised exhilaration as they dove past Ester again in the other direction: Asher's body was much lighter and quicker than they were used to, and with Barghest's fierce energy driving it, it didn't matter how fast it might tire. Any cost could be paid later, after this was done.

Asher felt the cost now—felt the gasping of her breath, the screaming strain in her muscles—and, unlike Barghest, knew what those sensations meant and what warnings they signified. Her body wanted to stop, and she wanted desperately to make it stop, to seize back control from the invader—

But she had promised she would not. She had *promised*

she would not. Base survival impulses came from the body. The soul could ignore them for a greater cause, and as Barghest pushed her body past its limits she shoved herself as far back as she could, her whole self trembling with the effort of maintaining its own absence.

And as she watched from within, somehow, impossibly, her body—her fragile overextended human body—spun once again behind Ester, caught them in the back of the knees and knocked them flat on their face.

Ester screamed in frustration and flipped themself over on all four arms, like a crab. But Barghest, it seemed, had been waiting for this. In a quick motion, they slipped in close and brought the point of Svanik's knife into the crack in Ester's carapace where their helmet met the front of their armor breastplate.

Asher's arms tensed with Barghest's intention to push forward the killing blow.

And tensed, and tensed, and stayed tense, and did not move.

ASHER'S MOUTH TWISTED as she stared at me, her chin and forehead tight with anger. It was an expression I'd never seen on her before. She looked the way I felt most of the time, but could never show. She could have killed me already, and from the way she looked, she wanted to. I couldn't figure out why she hadn't.

With that expression on her face, and all her curly hair shaved off, I wouldn't have recognized her in the street. Only the zit on her chin was the same, and the collection of bruises, and I knew none of those things were permanent either. It was amazing, really, how human faces changed.

And, as I watched, her face changed again. The twist in her mouth loosened, the eyes narrowed nervously, and suddenly she was recognizably Asher: stressed, distressed, upset, but not angry. Not the way she'd been a moment ago—or the way *someone* had been a moment ago. Someone who knew how I fought; who had taken advantage of every weakness in my training to do what no unaltered human should have been able to do, and defeat a Dedicate.

It didn't make any sense. I said it anyway: "Barghest."

"Yes," said Asher. "They're here." As if they were about to pull up a chair to join a party, rather than lurking somewhere behind her naked human eyes.

The gods were laughing at me again, probably. Had Barghest, the perfect Dedicate, ever even wanted to feel something with human skin?

"How?"

"Why don't you tell me first," said Asher, "why you lied to me?" There was a glint of anger in her face again now—different, I thought, than the rage that had radiated out of her earlier. But anger all the same. "You gave Barghest explanations, but not me. I want them now. You said you saved my life so I could be useful. All right. But you didn't have to talk to me, you didn't have to pretend that you were Vapenzi, so why—"

"I didn't lie," I said. "I *am* Gedank." I didn't owe her anything, but it was an opportunity to stall; with a knife at my throat, and Barghest's anger in Asher's eyes, I'd be a fool not to take it.

And I could see, also, that it mattered to Asher, and I'd be a fool to miss that opportunity, too. I didn't *want* to miss it.

I breathed, and heard the clink of metal as my carapace

hit the knife. "Everything I told you was the truth, actually. My mother's Gedank, but she was Cesteli, too. She even used to believe in your stupid war. Until she came back from the front, and found out that your fucking gods had stolen her kid while she was gone."

My mother had done everything she could. After she'd broken me out of the Holiest House, she couldn't risk staying in Cesteli. The bargain she'd made for asylum in Levasta gave their army the opportunity to train against a half-complete Dedicate, and me as much freedom as I could ever have. Still, as hard as she'd tried, there were some things she couldn't do anything about. I would be in this body for the rest of my life. I would only ever look human to my enemies. I would never smile at my mother, or anyone else. I would never feel anything on my skin.

Although somehow now Barghest did.

And Barghest said, now, wearily: "So your mother turned her back on her country and her vows for a single child of her body. I expect you think that's admirable."

I felt the knife scratch the surface of my flesh under the carapace, but still it didn't go any further.

I stared up at Asher's face. I imagined reaching up and popping the zit on her chin, both of us feeling that sharp, simple pain. How could Barghest stand to stay here, knees on my metal body, hands on a metal knife, instead of running off to touch every other thing that they could with her fingers?

I did reach up, then, after all. I couldn't feel it, but they could. I put my own iron hand up to Asher's face, watched her startle, and said, with all the confidence I had, "She doesn't want to kill me, does she?"

Asher didn't take her eyes off me, but when she spoke, it wasn't to me. "They did save my life."

"She," I said. It felt strange to say in Cestelenzi; I'd only ever had a gender in Levastan. "Me. I did. Though I don't know how much good it'll do, if your generals find out what you and the Sergeant are now. I bet they won't like that at all. Will they, Barghest?"

She didn't answer out loud, but I could see the rapid shifts behind her eyes, the twisting tension in her mouth. Barghest had no practice in hiding emotions on a palette as clear as a human face. They were arguing; they were distracted. There would be no better time than this.

With all the abruptness that Barghest had taught me, I used my lower arm to knock the knife away. As it went spinning into the air, I leaped up and threw her body to the ground.

She—or Barghest—was back up a moment later, but it didn't matter. They wouldn't catch me by surprise again, and without surprise they didn't have a hope. We faced each other across the snow, me, and the girl I'd saved, and the person behind her eyes that I'd betrayed.

"I got under your skin a little, didn't I?" I said to both of them. It was a prayer, in a way, a Gedank kind of prayer; you said the world you wanted to live in, and behaved like it was real, so the gods would make it so. "You can't see it the way you did before. The two of you won't last long back in your army. I'll bet you anything. When you've figured it out, come back to Green Adam and send up a signal. Maybe I'll still be here."

Then I turned and fled, knowing they wouldn't follow.

Barghest was almost glad of the time it took to get back to the rendezvous point. They had to focus on the mental map that Asher had provided them, on making sure they didn't miss any landmarks and that none of the other Dedicates had difficulty moving in the snow.

It made it easier to ignore Asher's sense of failure, a gloomy fog pervading both their thoughts. It made it possible to put aside the moment when they'd had their knife at Ester's throat and Asher's hesitation had held their hands back.

They could have pushed through it. They almost had. But Asher was still their commander, and so it was lucky that they did not have time to replay the moment again in their head, with the taste of Asher's self-blame in their throat.

It was deep into the night by the time they all made it back. The Dedicates tromped into the campsite one by one, and the quiet, wet sound of Svanik's coughing—a sound Barghest had been trying to stop themselves from hearing through Asher's ears all the way down the mountain—was suddenly drowned out by heavy footsteps and clanking metal.

Tvell went right over to Svanik. "I didn't realize it was so bad," they said, sounding shocked. "Are they—"

"I thought about amputating here," said Firzen. Their voice was leached of anything besides exhaustion. "But they wouldn't survive it. The Commander says it's only two days' march from here to the army, so there might be a chance—" They broke off, and then said, simply, "I'm glad you're all back."

"We'll go soon." Asher stood up from where she'd been sitting cross-legged on the ground. "We'll let everyone have a chance to eat and sit for a little, and then we'll go."

She hadn't slept since their fight with Titan. Barghest could feel her exhaustion, but they didn't say anything.

Svanik didn't have much time. She was right to make the choice. Barghest would carry her, if necessary.

"Hey," said Dreizen, suddenly, "where's Titan?"

Asher flinched. "Gone."

Dreizen stared at her. "*Gone?*"

Asher shook her head, as if to clear it, and then said, in a firmer tone: "She—she wasn't what she seemed. She was a spy here to steal a command plate, but..."

As she reached into her pockets, Barghest realized what she was about to do. *Wait,* they thought, and felt her hand stutter before it touched the jagged shards of the command plate, but she didn't stop. She pulled the shards out of her pocket and held them out for all the others to see.

"She changed her mind. She didn't steal it. She broke it. Um, as you see."

They deserve to know, she said, to Barghest.

Barghest didn't contradict her; still, they wished she had waited a little longer, and given them both time to plan. They tried to read what reactions they could in the shocked stillness of the Dedicates around them. Asher was looking too, and for a moment Barghest saw themself as she saw them—a grim, battered statue—before her gaze passed on.

As the silence stretched, Asher cleared her throat. "Um, so—we all have a choice to make, about—"

"And where did Titan go?" Cascabela demanded, at almost the same time. Their voice boomed. "Did you kill them?"

"*No.*" Asher's tone was defensive. "I didn't—no. She ran away. She's probably somewhere on the mountain still."

"Good," said Cascabela, and pushed themself to their feet.

With a dull sense of inevitability, Barghest stood as well.

Firzen looked alarmed. "If you're going to fight them by yourself—"

"Fight them!" It was the first time Barghest had ever heard Cascabela laugh. "Why would I do that?"

"Don't be an idiot," said Dirk. "They'll just put your chip in another plate, and then where will you be?"

Cascabela's head turned thoughtfully towards Asher. Barghest's muscles tensed in preparation. If it came to a fight, here and now—they thought they knew who would jump which way, but you could never be sure. Things could go very badly very quickly.

It's all right, said Asher in their head, and out loud, she said, "You didn't let me finish? I did mean a choice." She stepped past Barghest, towards Cascabela, and put their chip in their hand.

Cascabela's hand closed over it, but they didn't step back. Barghest readied themself. Potential violence hung in the air like a pressure system.

Then Cascabela lifted a rueful shoulder and turned away.

They passed quickly out of the range of Barghest's peripheral vision. Barghest didn't turn their head to watch them go. They felt as hollow inside as they looked through Asher's eyes. They had failed Cascabela, over and over, and now they'd never have another chance.

Asher didn't watch Cascabela's departure either. She turned to the others, her voice trembling a little, and said, "Well? Anyone else?"

"Sir," said Firzen, sounding appalled, "we're *Dedicates.*"

At the same time, Svanik spoke, for the first time in

hours. Their voice rasped, but neither Barghest nor Asher could make out the words.

"What?" said Asher.

Tvell was the closest. They leaned down, then looked back at Asher. "They said—ah—'get rid of all the fucking chips you have left.' And, um, I agree with them. Sir."

"*Tvell*," said Firzen.

"We'll go back, of course!" added Tvell hastily. "We need to help Svanik, and—Firzen's right, we're Dedicated, of course we want to serve the country and the gods—" The phrases were said rote, without much conviction. "But—don't bring any chips back with you. Please."

"Dirk?" said Asher. "Dreizen? What do you think?"

Dirk shrugged, and leaned back against the mountainside.

"I'm not going to leave Svanik like this," said Dreizen. "So Tvell's plan works for me." And then, because Dreizen was Dreizen, they kept talking: "But if it wasn't for the others, sir, I'd go with Cascabela."

Dreizen, thought Barghest, wearily, could use any number of lessons in discretion—and as they thought that, Tvell said, in tones of deep frustration, "Why would you *tell* her that?"

"I thought she should know." Dreizen shrugged, then looked around. "So is that it? I'm going to make some gruel."

In Barghest's head, Asher thought, *I'm sorry. I didn't ask you what you wanted.*

Barghest didn't answer. There didn't seem a point.

Asher persisted: *Your chip was one of the last ones I found. I could have let it stay lost. Maybe it would all have been all right.*

Barghest wondered if she wanted self-punishment or reassurance. *You should sit,* they told her instead. Asher's legs were still shaky, her muscles swollen and stiff after the desperation of their pursuit. They would have to learn more about her limits. *Rest while you can.*

They settled back down on the ground themself, cross-legged, and Asher obediently came to sit next to them. Her eyes drifted towards the horizon—the way they would be traveling tomorrow, when they left the mountain—and Barghest looked there, too, so their fields of vision almost overlapped in a slightly unfocused haze of green.

You jumped after me. Asher's thought shattered the stillness between them like a shout. *During the earthquake, you took the worst of my fall. That's how you dented your back.*

Barghest's breath hissed in. They hadn't thought she remembered that.

I don't—but it makes sense.

It was, Barghest thought, carefully, *my duty.* It seemed important that she understand this. They had barely known her, then, but a Dedicate was a shield. Sacrifice was what they were for.

I know. Asher closed her eyes; Barghest's vision focused. *Still, that's part of why...*

You're in command. You made a decision. You needn't justify yourself to me.

She made a noise that might have been a laugh. *I don't think we can even pretend it's like that now.*

A flash of memory, relentlessly echoed: the easy command Barghest had taken of her body. The way it had felt for Barghest to control her; the way it had felt for Asher to hold herself back; how dangerously close they had come, at the crucial moment, to crushing her resistance and forcing her hand.

Asher went on, tentatively: *Were you listening when I asked Firzen, earlier? They didn't trust themself to try and take your chip out of me now that the godstone's begun to bind. But they said, maybe an army surgeon, once we get back—*

You shouldn't tell them. Barghest cut her off, and regretted it a little when they felt Asher's mind whip back at the force and speed with which they had severed the thought.

They had been putting aside, as much as they could, that moment of failure when Ester had fled. They had mostly been able to forget the way the knife had felt in their hands, but the last thing she'd said still rang in their ears.

You shouldn't ever tell them, they repeated, more gently. They could feel the sea of guilt and anxiety that was always right below the surface of her thoughts, and offered their certainty to her like a spar. *You can't tell them anything that's happened here. Ester was right. The high command wouldn't like it.*

It didn't take Asher long to grasp the logic. She opened her eyes, and looked back towards the others, seeing what the Cesteli army would see: five Dedicates whose behavior could no longer be predicted or controlled. Five weapons who could now aim themselves.

Dedicates were a shield: for the country, for the sisters— and for each other, as nobody else could be. Asher was not a Dedicate, but she was as close now as anybody else could come. And she was a quick study.

I only promised to get them off the mountain—but I guess it can't stop there, can it? Maybe it was stupid to ever think it could.

144

It could have, Barghest told her. *But you chose duty, too.*

Something in her eased at the approval, the way it always did. She sighed, and leaned her head against Barghest's shoulder. *Well—you're a good teacher.*

Barghest sat very still. They had always known their machinery gave off heat, but not, before, what it felt like.

It turned out, it was good to be warm.

IT WOULD BE easy enough to lie about what had happened here. Even though I had failed, I was still more valuable to Levasta now than I had been before I left. I'd used a command plate. I could provide more details about how it worked. And I knew how to fight against other Dedicates, where to find their weak spots. How to kill them better and faster.

I could go back to my adopted country. I could reassure my mother; she would be worrying. I could be surrounded by normal human faces, and all of them would look at me like an *incredibly* useful monster.

Alternately, I could just become a horrible hermit on the world's worst mountain.

I was making a fire on the second day, still trying to decide, when I heard heavy footsteps behind me.

I turned, already expecting to see Barghest, half-dreading another fight, and half-excited for it; at least that way something would *happen*—

But instead it was one of the others. A Dedicate with a limp upper right arm, and a thoroughly bashed-up lower one.

"Um?" I said, stupidly.

Cascabela went around to the other side of my fire and

sat down as if they belonged there. They opened up the compartment in their working arm, pulled out a spoon, and started placidly helping themself to my gruel.

"*Um*," I said.

"I heard you broke our command plate," said Cascabela. I truly hadn't thought it was possible for their voice to sound this cheerful.

"I... did," I said.

"All right," said Cascabela. They slid their drinking straw inside the grille over their mouth, took a long slurp of gruel, and pulled it out again. "Plenty of troops come this way, you know. Over the mountain."

"...Oh?" I said.

"Well," said Cascabela. "How would you like to do it again?"

They were a Dedicate, like me. They couldn't smile any more than I could.

But I think they would have, if they could; and if they did, I would have smiled back.

ACKNOWLEDGMENTS

WITH TREMENDOUS THANKS to all the people without whom this book would not exist:

Debi, Jo, Lynne, Lexie, and Sandry, for the clone feelings.

Kristin MacDonough, Freya Marske, and Kelsey, for the regular check-ins, constant encouragement, and occasional kicks in the pants in November 2018.

Meredith Rose Schorr, for the handholding through the Process.

Alex Schaffner, Ari Brezina, A. A. McNamara, and Shoshana Flax, who read far too many drafts and made it infinitely better every time.

Michael Lin, Sophia Kalman, Sophie Herron, Ren Hutchings, and Bethany Jacobs, who brought fresh eyes to the almost-final version, and promised me that it more or less made sense without having already read far too many drafts.

My incredible agent, Bridget Smith, and my extremely wise editor, Amy Borsuk, both of whom engaged with and improved the text on every level.

The rest of the wonderful team at Rebellion, including Jim Killen, who saw the potential in the book; Jess Gofton, who made sure other people would want to read it; and Sam Gretton, who gave it a beautiful face.

All of my brilliant and talented friends, both the ones who live in the groupchats – outfit courtroom, box comrades, the lizards, MIAP niners, Team B – and the ones I'm lucky enough to see in three-dimensional space, who make every day a little easier to get through with good takes, bad jokes, constant non sequiturs and endless solidarity.

My parents, brother and sister-in-law, who never doubted I could do it, thus making sure I had to prove them right.

Sarah Emily, whose constant encouragement and support has been essential to everything I've managed to write since 2009.

And last but always, always first, my beautiful fiancee Beth; getting to marry you is far and away the best thing about this year.

ABOUT THE AUTHOR

REBECCA FRAIMOW is an author and archivist living in Boston. Her short fiction has recently appeared in PodCastle, The Fantasist, and Consolation Songs: Optimistic Speculative Fiction for a Time of Pandemic, among other venues. Her short story in Consolation Songs, "This Is New Gehesran Calling," appeared on the longlist for the 2021 Hugo Award.

FIND US ONLINE!

www.rebellionpublishing.com

/solarisbooks   /solarisbks   /solarisbooks

SIGN UP TO OUR NEWSLETTER!

rebellionpublishing.com/newsletter

YOUR REVIEWS MATTER!

Enjoy this book? Got something to say?

Leave a review on Amazon, Goodreads or with your
favourite bookseller and let the world know!

THE DIFFICULT LOVES
OF MARIA MAKILING

WAYNE SANTOS

"REPLETE WITH SNAPPY DIALOGUE, THIS IS FUN
AND FRESH" – *PUBLISHERS WEEKLY* ON *THE CHIMERA CODE*

SATELLITES

◐ SOLARISBOOKS.COM

THESE LIFELESS THINGS

PREMEE MOHAMED

"GASP-OUT-LOUD ASTONISHING"
– CHARLIE JANE ANDERS ON *BENEATH THE RISING*

SATELLITES

⊙ SOLARISBOOKS.COM

POLLEN FROM A
FUTURE HARVEST

DEREK KÜNSKEN

"KÜNSKEN'S VIVID WORLDBUILDING IS A
KNOCKOUT" – *PUBLISHERS WEEKLY*

SATELLITES

SOLARISBOOKS.COM

KID WOLF AND
KRAKEN BOY

SAM J. MILLER

SATELLITES

⊙ SOLARISBOOKS.COM

UNTO THE GODLESS
WHAT LITTLE REMAINS

MÁRIO COELHO

SATELLITES

SOLARISBOOKS.COM

THE SURF

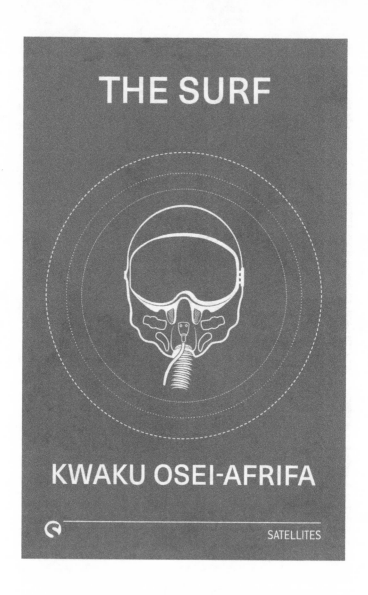

KWAKU OSEI-AFRIFA

SATELLITES

CPSIA information can be obtained
at www.ICGtesting.com
Printed in the USA
JSHW021159020423
39736JS00005B/24

9 781786 189882